'Damn it, you numbskull, nobody's the least bit interested in us as actors. They want to see us together. That's what I meant when I said it's not going to be good enough. Everybody's expectations are so crazy...''

Shannon's words stumbled to a halt as a crooked smile flickered across Cade's face. 'What is it?'

He crossed the room slowly and paused beside her chair. She watched as he took the empty glass from her hand and set it on the table.

'Let me show you something,' he said, twining his fingers through hers.

'Show me what?' Her voice was wary, but she let him pull her slowly to her feet. 'Cade?'

'Nobody's going to be disappointed,' he said, drawing her towards him. 'Not anybody, Shannon. I guarantee it.'

'Cade, please...'

His hands tangled in the cascade of her hair as he bent his head to hers and her whispered plea was lost against his mouth.

LOVESCENES

BY

SANDRA MARTON

MILLS & BOON LIMITED
ETON HOUSE   18-24 PARADISE ROAD
RICHMOND   SURREY   TW9 1SR

First published in Great Britain 1987
by Mills & Boon Limited

© Sandra Myles 1987

Australian copyright 1987
Philippine copyright 1987
This edition 1987

ISBN 0 263 75816 8

Set in Times Roman 10 on 11 pt.
01-1187-57211 C

Printed and bound in Great Britain by
Collins, Glasgow

For RDM and MIM,
with love and laughter,
gearshifts and heat graphs.

CHAPTER ONE

THE oversized bed was a dimly lit oasis centred in the surrounding darkness. Its soft pillows and down quilt were the boundaries of the universe for the man and woman lying, limbs tangled and intertwined, amid the silken sheets. The soft strains of Vivaldi's *Four Seasons* filled the room, its delicate rhythms a counterpoint to the abandonment of the couple on the bed. The woman's eyes were closed, her thick, black lashes lying like dark shadows against her pale skin. The man beside her smiled and touched his lips to her slender throat.

'I want you, darling,' he groaned, his hand roaming over the curving line of her hip, outlined softly beneath the pale peach sheet. 'I've wanted you from the moment I saw you.'

The woman sighed. 'Yes,' she whispered, 'yes...'

'You were all I could think about tonight. I thought of this moment a hundred times. Tell me you thought about it, too.'

'It's true,' she said softly. 'I couldn't keep my mind on anything else...'

The laundry, she thought, tangling her hands in the man's thick, blond hair. God, I forgot to pick it up last night! And my blue silk dress is still at the cleaners...

The man shifted his weight and drew her against his chest. 'I've never felt this way before,' he said.

'Darling,' she whispered. Her eyes fluttered open and she smiled. 'I don't know what's happening to me...'

...aside from the fact that I don't have anything to wear tonight. By the time I finally get away from here, the cleaners and the laundry will both be closed. Well, I can always wear jeans or my grey wool trousers. It's not as if I'm going somewhere special . . .

'I'm going to make you know the meaning of passion,' the man said huskily. He caught a handful of the woman's long, black hair and leaned towards her. 'You'll never forget this night, darling.'

She smiled again and clasped the back of his head with one hand. 'Neither of us will,' she promised.

She pulled his head down to hers and their mouths met in a long kiss. The grey wool trousers, she thought. She was only going to dinner with her agent—they'd probably go to that little Italian place near the studio—but Claire had mentioned that she wanted to make a quick stop after dinner. She had to see a new client or something . . . She grunted softly as the man rolled his body across hers. There was something sharp in the damned mattress and it was digging into her hip. And the pillow was harder than a bag of cement . . .

'Come on, Shannon! The least you can do is pay attention during a seduction.'

The deep voice broke the woman's line of thought. She rose on her elbows and stared into the darkness.

'What's the matter?' she asked hesitantly. 'Did I muff my lines?'

'No,' the voice admitted. 'It's . . . Harry, bring up the lights, would you? OK, everybody. We'll take a five-minute break.'

The couple on the bed broke apart as the studio lights blazed on and the music shut off abruptly. The man grinned and sat up, the sheets falling below his waist and past his baggy seat pants.

'God,' he groaned, scratching his bare chest, 'I think I'm allergic to this damned quilt. It's got to be the feathers. The sacrifices we make for *All Our Tomorrows*! Who said daytime TV drama wasn't a legitimate art, anyhow?'

Shannon Padgett smiled as she scrambled to her feet. 'Probably the last poor actress who spent an hour lying on her back in this studio, Tony.' She tugged the straps of her flesh-coloured bodysuit up over her arms and then rubbed the small of her back. 'This isn't a mattress, it's a rock pile.'

Tony Richmond grinned and flicked his dark blond hair from his forehead. 'Do me a favour, sweetie. Don't let any of my fans hear you say that, hmm? All those little housewives out in TV land would die if they knew you were thinking about your bad back while I made passionate love to you.' A grin curved wickedly on his handsome face. 'I can promise you that my date last night didn't think about anything so mundane.'

'You'd better hope the mikes are off when you say something like that,' Shannon laughed. She snatched up her short, terry-cloth robe and slipped it on. 'Maybe it's just as well this was only a rehearsal.'

Tony turned towards the man standing beside the sound boom. 'You wouldn't let anything like than happen to me, would you, Jerry? You're too good a director to let me fall on my face.'

The director of New York's longest running television daytime drama nodded. 'I'm too good to let *All Our Tomorrows* fall on its face,' he said carefully. 'Why don't you take a quick shower, Tony? You'll scratch yourself raw if you don't get those feathers off you.'

Tony Richmond nodded. 'Thanks, Jerry. I'll be ready in five mintues.'

Jerry Crawford waved his hand in the air. 'Yeah, take your time. I want to talk to Shannon, anyway.'

Shannon Padgett arched her dark eyebrows. 'That sounds ominous,' she said, hoping she sounded less concerned than she felt. 'Is there a problem, Mr Crawford?'

The director smiled at her and draped his arm across her shoulders. 'That's what I wanted to ask you,

Shannon. And please call me Jerry. We're informal here. You should know that by now.'

She nodded, thinking she should know a great deal after two weeks on the set, but the truth was that she still felt like an outsider. Who wouldn't? she thought. Most of the cast and crew had been together for years. In a business as chancy as acting, that was rare. It was also wonderful—and, thanks mostly to luck, she was being given a chance to become a more permanent member of that cast. What had begun as a bit part that was supposed to last a month might be turning into something more substantial, something that might last at least until spring. But not if the director was displeased with her, she thought, glancing sideways at the man. Not if he decided she didn't really fit the part...

'I guess I forgot to turn my face to the camera after Tony rolls over me,' she said quickly. 'I'm sorry, Mr... Jerry. I'll do it right the next time.'

Jerry Crawford shook his head. 'No, that's not it, Shannon,' he said, squeezing her shoulder lightly. 'Look, you know what the writers had in mind for your characters, don't you? You and Tony meet, the sparks fly, and you end up in bed together.' He paused and his arm dropped from Shannon's shoulder. 'The thing is, I don't feel those sparks, my dear. You and Tony go through all the motions, but nothing comes across. No desire, no wanting, no passion.'

Shannon sighed. 'I see,' she said slowly, running her hand through her dark hair. 'Maybe if I understood more about why we fall into bed so fast... The script has us meeting at a cocktail party and then, the next thing anybody knows, we're there, in that bed.' She waved her hand in the general direction of the set and shrugged her shoulders. 'That's not in keeping with the character I play, Jerry. She's a strong, modern won...n, yes, but that doesn't mean she'd end up in bed with a man when they've barely exchanged names.'

Her words drifted into the echoing silence of the high-ceilinged sound stage. I went too far, she thought, glancing at the man beside her. He looked—amused? Annoyed? Well, whatever that twist to his lips meant, it wasn't good. Just do what Crawford asks, her agent had said. And don't overdo the Stanislavsky bit, Shannon. This guy's got to get a show on tape every day and rehearse stuff still coming down the pike. He's not into your 'inner space' exercises. If he says you feel happy, that's how you feel. You don't need to know why.

'Look, forget I said all that, Mr...Jerry,' Shannon said hastily. 'I'm a pro and I can give you what you want. Just give me another chance.'

The director laughed softly. 'You poor child,' he said. 'Did you think I was going to fire you? Shannon, dear, part of the reason we enlarged your part was because we've had such good audience reaction to you...' A peal of laughter cut across the sound stage and both Shannon and the director looked across the room. 'You're a good actress, Shannon,' Crawford said, putting his arm around her again. 'You impressed all of us when you auditioned for that other part last year.'

Rima's part, Shannon thought, glancing across the room again. She'd tried out for it almost eleven months ago, but Rima had got the part instead and what was more, they'd changed it to suit her. She had only one scene to do today and Jerry had already taken her through it. The woman's performance had been wooden and emotionless, just as it would be later when it was taped for tomorrow's show. The director's gaze followed Shannon's and he nodded.

'I know what you're thinking,' he said. 'And you're right, Shannon. I am, indeed, demanding more of you than I do of Rima. But only because I know you can give more than you have. Do you understand?'

What he really meant was that Rima didn't have to give anything more than her name, Shannon thought with a trace of bitterness. Rima Dalton had been a model when she was ten years old. Her hauntingly strange, child-woman face had been on every magazine cover in the western world. When she reached thirty, the close-ups that had been so kind to her exotic young features became a cruel parody. It was then that Rima had decided to become an actress, and, with a name that generated publicity, that was easy. The producers of *All Our Tomorrows* had rewritten the role Shannon had read for, changing it so they could cast Rima as an older, stereotypical soap opera villainess. The role didn't require much talent and, thanks to the narrow confines of the television screen and careful editing, Rima had become a star. Not an actress—at least, not in Shannon's eyes—but a star.

Shannon nodded her head. 'Yes, I understand,' she said carefully. 'I'll get it right the next time.'

'You have to feel the passion, Shannon. You meet this guy, you talk for an hour or so, he takes you back to his apartment, and wham! the feeling between you is so strong, so powerful, that you fly in the face of every convention. You fall into his arms and into his bed.' Jerry's arm slid around her shoulders again and he gave her an encouraging hug. 'You and Tony have to make the audience understand your character's behaviour. What I want is…is Tracy and Hepburn, Taylor and Burton, the feeling that you got watching that film a couple of years ago, you know, *Body Heat*. Did you see it? There's a scene between the two main characters the first time they go to bed together that just blows the audience away.'

She nodded again. 'Yes, I know the scene,' she said. She certainly did. She'd felt like a voyeur watching it. It had been hard to believe that the man and woman on screen were acting, even for someone with her training in the theatre. 'All right, Jerry, I know what you want. I…'

'What the hell's all that about?' the director demanded, turning towards the front of the studio. A small crowd had gathered around the door and, as they watched, more people joined it, until finally Shannon and Jerry Crawford were the only ones at the far end of the huge room. 'Just what I need,' he said sharply, taking Shannon's elbow. 'A party of VIPs out slumming.'

Shannon hurried along beside the man, her bare feet padding softly across the floor. As they neared the door, she could hear the babble of excited voices and see the smiles on the faces of the people gathered there. Two of the cameramen were staring at the door as if royalty had just entered. The script girl and the make-up woman—all the females, in fact—had embarrassingly stupid grins on their faces. The gathering parted as Jerry Crawford shouldered his way through it, and Shannon had no choice but to follow since he was still holding her arm.

'Come on, people,' he said, 'get back to work. We have a final shoot for tomorrow's show in a little while, and I want to finish rehearsing Tony and Shannon.' Crawford drew in his breath and a smile wreathed his face. 'Well, I'll be damned!' he said softly. 'Cade Morgan! I didn't expect to see you today.' Shannon fell back as Crawford's hand dropped from her elbow and he moved towards a man in the centre of the crowd. 'Why didn't you let us know you were coming, Cade? I'd have had the welcoming committee out.'

The man separated himself from the group surrounding him and stepped forward. 'That was precisely why I didn't,' he said pleasantly, taking Crawford's outstretched hand in his. 'I didn't want to interrupt your normal work-day.'

'My God,' Tony's voice drawled softly in Shannon's ear, 'it's Cade Morgan.' He shook his head and droplets of water rained on to her face. 'Jesus, isn't he a gorgeous son of a bitch?'

Usually, Shannon laughed and corrected Tony's overblown adjectives, but this time she simply nodded. It was hard to quarrel with Tony's description, although she wouldn't have used the word to describe Cade Morgan. Gorgeous was a word that conjured up images of softness, and there was nothing soft about this man. He was a world-famous musician and she'd seen him dozens of times before—on television, in magazines and newspapers—but never in person.

'Did you see him on the tube with the Boston Pops the other night?' Tony whispered. 'How can a guy head a group like the Marauders one day and play classical guitar the next?'

It was an interesting question, Shannon thought, staring at Cade Morgan, one which had intrigued music critics for years. Only Morgan's admiring fans asked no questions. They were content simply to pack his concerts and buy his records, whether they were blues, rock, or classical. She had, indeed, seen his appearance with the symphony. Dressed in black tie, he'd been a handsome, imposing figure; now, standing in the studio, he was all that and more, although the formal dress had been replaced by a black leather motorcycle jacket, tight, faded jeans, and dusty black leather boots.

Jerry was leading Cade Morgan through the little group of admirers. They were still talking, although every now and then Morgan paused and smiled at someone, shaking hands and exchanging pleasantries.

'Somebody's going to whip out a piece of paper and ask him for an autograph any second,' Tony whispered. He chuckled softly. 'You'd never think we were a bunch of pros, would you?'

No, Shannon thought, you certainly wouldn't. Even Rima was gushing like a schoolgirl. She glanced at her watch and grimaced. Was Jerry going to bow and scrape to the man, too? Clearly, they weren't going to be held to the director's usually rigid five-minute break—although it wasn't rigid when Rima wanted to take time out for coffee or to have her hair fixed or her make-up touched up or . . . Something knotted inside her as she watched—and yes, there was the first request for an autograph. Somebody had picked up a script and thrust it in front of Morgan's face.

Tony moved closer to her. 'Can you imagine the future I'd have if I looked like that?' He grinned and shrugged his shoulders. 'I'm not modest, love—you know that—and I like what I see in my mirror, but there's something about that man. You'd think Hollywood would have picked him up by now, wouldn't you? Jeez, if I were in his shoes, I'd be beating the studios off with a stick.' Shannon looked up sharply. Tony, too, she thought with disgust. 'Do you think Jerry will introduce us?' he asked. 'I'm not sure the peasants get a shot at visiting celebrities . . .'

'We're not peasants,' she said sharply. 'And I'm not going to stand around waiting. Cade Morgan is a guitar player, that's all. That's why Hollywood hasn't bothered with him. They have more sense than we do. Why people with stage credits and years of training should make fools of themselves over someone like that . . .'

Her words seemed to echo through the sound stage, bouncing off the walls of the cavernous room. Shannon's face turned crimson with embarrassment. Somehow, what she'd intended to be a whisper had turned out to be a roar. Every head in the room turned towards her; every eye fastened on her.

'Bye, bye, kid,' Tony whispered in a half-groan. 'It's been nice knowing you.'

She felt him move away from her. In fact, everyone seemed to have moved away from her—except for Cade Morgan. He had turned at the first sound of her voice and now he was standing a few feet away, smiling politely.

'Were you speaking to me?' he asked.

Shannon swallowed drily. His voice was low and husky, but she was sure it carried into every nook of the room.

'No,' she said finally, 'no, I wasn't.'

Cade Morgan smiled and moved towards her. 'About me, then. You were speaking about me, Miss . . . ?'

She tilted her chin up and her eyes met his. 'My name is Padgett,' she said clearly. 'Shannon Padgett.' He was smiling, but his eyes were cold. What colour were they, anyway? Blue? Black? Indigo, perhaps . . . 'And I didn't mean what I said—not quite the way it sounded.'

Morgan stopped inches from her. 'Really?' He grinned lazily. 'You mean, you don't have stage credits?' She shook her head and his smile broadened. 'Then, perhaps you'll explain which part you didn't mean the way it sounded, Miss Padgett. That you've had years of training? Did you mean that?'

Shannon closed her eyes briefly and took a deep breath. In the two weeks she'd been working here, she'd never heard the studio this quiet. Like a graveyard, she thought, flinching inwardly at the simile, for she might be at her own funeral. Her glance flickered to her director. Jerry was standing just behind Cade Morgan, and the expression on his face was unreadable.

'I'd appreciate it if you wouldn't play cat and mouse with me, Mr Morgan,' she said evenly. 'You know what I said as well as I do. And I apologise. It was rude. It was insulting. It was . . .'

'It was true,' Cade Morgan said easily. 'At least, part of it was. I am a *guitar player*,' he said, giving the words the special emphasis she'd afforded them. 'I take it you think that's not a respectable occupation?'

'I've already said I was sorry, Mr Morgan. I . . .'

'You made it sound like an obscenity, Miss Padgett.'

She looked past him again, silently pleading with the director to interrupt, but Jerry's face was a blank.

'Mr Morgan . . .'

'I'm a musician, Miss Padgett. I've never pretended to be anything else. And I'm as proud of that as you are of being an actress.' His indigo gaze drifted over her, and she felt as if he'd undressed her and left her naked and defenceless. 'You are an actress, aren't you?' he asked, his eyes lingering on the long expanse of bare leg visible beneath her thigh-length robe. She resisted the urge to try and tug it down, but she winced with humiliation and Morgan grinned. 'Although I can think of other ways you could earn your living.'

Someone in the crowd tittered nervously and Shannon's head snapped up. 'I beg your pardon?' she said coldly.

Morgan shrugged his shoulders. 'As a dancer, for example,' he said pleasantly. 'Or a model...' He reached out and touched one finger lightly to her cheek. 'What did you think I meant, Miss Padgett?'

Her skin burned where he'd touched it and she tilted her face away from his hand.

'I couldn't care less,' she said evenly. 'I'm an actress, Mr Morgan, and——'

'And a damned good one,' Jerry Crawford said suddenly, walking towards them. He smiled broadly and clapped Cade Morgan on the back. 'Shannon's one of our new cast members, Cade. She's playing the part of the girl who shows up in Clover City claiming to be the Dunbar heiress.'

Cade nodded. 'I should have figured that, Jerry. Sure, the one who seduces the guy at the party.'

Shannon stiffened imperceptibly. Somehow, it irritated her no end to learn that her director had discussed her part with this man. After all, he had nothing to do with *All Our Tomorrows*. In fact, he had nothing to do with acting. And he certainly didn't know her character, she thought grimly.

'She doesn't seduce anybody,' Shannon said to Jerry. 'Not Alana Dunbar.'

But it was Cade Morgan who answered. 'Sure she does, Miss Padgett. She meets this guy—what's his name, Jimmy or Johnny...'

'Johnny,' she said automatically. 'Look, Jerry...'

'And she turns on the heat and he winds up in bed with her.'

'Mr Morgan, you've obviously never read the script. She does no such thing. She...'

'She charms the hell out of this guy...'

Shannon clucked her tongue impatiently. 'That's not what happens. I go to the party, I meet this man, and he sweeps me off my feet. When he kisses me...'

Cade Morgan snorted. 'When he kisses you? Jesus, Miss Padgett, you sure as hell look old enough to know who kisses who.' He turned to the director and scowled. 'I'm right, aren't I, Jerry? She kisses him, doesn't she?'

Jerry Crawford shrugged his shoulders. 'Don't ask me,' he said innocently. 'I don't remember.'

'That's ridiculous!' Shannon snapped. 'He kisses her. I should know, shouldn't I? I mean, it's my scene. And I certainly know whether someone's kissed me or I've kissed him. I...'

'Clearly, you don't, Miss Padgett,' Cade Morgan growled. Before Shannon could move, he wrapped one hand around the back of her head and drew her to him. 'This is what it's like when someone kisses you,' he said, and his mouth closed over hers.

Shannon's outraged cry was lost against Cade Morgan's hard mouth. She heard the startled gasp of the people watching them and then, for the thudding tick of a heartbeat, the room spun away from her. Her senses reeled under the sudden, unexpected assault, telling her that he smelled of leather and cold air, that his mouth tasted clean and sweet, that his grasp was like steel, that it was drawing her closer to him, so close that she could almost lean into him and close her eyes and...

Cade's hand dropped away from her as suddenly as it had brought her to him.

'Have you got it straight now, Miss Padgett?' he asked softly. 'That's what it feels like when you're kissed.'

Shannon's eyes met his. For a second, something seemed to glint in his incredible eyes... No, she thought, the only thing shining there was satisfaction. Of course he was satisfied—he'd repaid her insult, and he'd done it with interest. Carefully, she squared her shoulders.

'Really?' she asked in a voice that almost purred. 'Well, I guess I haven't been missing much, then.' The crowd murmured in delight and Cade Morgan's eyes narrowed. Don't push your luck, Padgett, Shannon told herself quickly. Exit, stage left, and do it fast. 'Jerry,' she said sweetly, turning to the director, 'I'll be in my dressing-room.'

She waited for Jerry to tell her not to bother, that all she had to do was pick up her pay cheque and leave the set for ever, but he simply smiled and nodded.

'Sure, Shannon,' he said agreeably. 'I'll call you when we need you.'

'Do that,' she said, as if she gave directors orders every day. Without so much as a glance at Cade Morgan, Shannon tossed her head and stalked across the stage, trying not to dwell on the fact that her bare legs probably ruined what she had wanted to be a regal effect.

But Cade Morgan was dwelling on it, at least, she thought he was. Why else would his low, wicked chuckle follow after her? It didn't make for a dramatic exit—and neither did the fact that she could still feel the imprint of the man's arrogant mouth against hers.

CHAPTER TWO

'ARE you sure you don't mind having dinner on the run, Shannon? I know you were probably looking forward to veal *piccata* at Luigi's.'

Shannon shook her head and shrugged free of her corduroy jacket. 'Luigi's veal *piccata* tonight means black coffee all day tomorrow,' she said with a grin. 'Believe me, Claire, I'm better off sticking with something less fattening. A salad, maybe.'

'You need more than that after working all day. Have a small steak along with it.' Claire Holden looked around the noisy restaurant and laughed softly. 'Although I don't think places like this know the meaning of the word small. Just look at the size of those portions, will you?'

Shannon nodded in agreement. 'This is the real world, Claire,' she said lightly. 'People eat real food in—where are we, anyway? Queens? Brooklyn?'

Her agent grinned and folded her hands on the red formica table. 'For shame, Shannon,' she teased. 'You've lived in New York long enough to know that the Nassau Coliseum is on Long Island. You know, just east of Queens . . .'

'And west of the moon,' Shannon laughed. 'Well, it might as well be. I never get a chance to get out of the city.'

'You're not supposed to,' Claire said. 'Up and coming actresses are supposed to spend all their time with their noses to the grindstone. Acting lessons, dancing lessons, exercise class . . .'

'"Up and coming,"' Shannon repeated wistfully. 'Why does that sound so much better than "struggling"?'

'Because you're not struggling, not any more. This part on *Tomorrows* is the break we waited for, sweetie. Good money, good lines, good exposure...'

'Don't remind me about the exposure part,' Shannon said, reaching towards a large muffin peeking out from a napkin-covered basket, 'not after I spent the whole afternoon playing hide and seek with Tony in that damned bed.' She shook her head imperceptibly and drew her hand back. 'Take my mind off *Tomorrows*, Claire. Tell me what we're doing here.'

'I already told you,' her agent said casually, smoothing a thick layer of butter on half a roll, 'I have to see some guy who's at the Coliseum tonight.' She popped the roll into her mouth. 'Delicious,' she said, her words muffled and uneven. 'I bet that muffin's even better.'

Shannon shook her head. 'Too many calories for me.' She folded her hands in her lap and smiled at the other woman. 'I thought they played hockey games at the Coliseum. Don't tell me you're representing hockey players now, Claire.'

'Can you just picture that?' the agent asked with a laugh. 'Not very likely. The only thing I know about hockey is that it's played with a chuck.'

Shannon burst out laughing. 'A puck,' she said. 'Even I know that much.'

The agent shrugged her shoulders and buttered the remaining piece of roll. 'You see? It's a good thing we're not here to see a hockey game.' She bit into the roll and chewed silently. 'They hold concerts here, too,' she said, swallowing the mouthful of bread. 'Matter of fact, there's one tonight.' She glanced at Shannon and then at the bread basket. 'I could have sworn I saw a cranberry muffin in there.'

'If you wanted to see a concert, we could have stayed in the city. There's a Chopin programme at the Lincoln Center tonight...'

Claire shook her head. 'This is business,' she said, poking at the rolls and muffins. 'Aha, there you are, you little devil. Thought you could escape me, huh?'

'Will you please give me a straight answer? Are you telling me you're here to watch a musician perform?'

Claire nodded.

'I didn't know you handled musicians.'

The agent sighed dramatically. 'Please, let's not talk about my sex life, OK? You know it only depresses me.'

'Come on,' Shannon laughed, 'you know what I meant. I thought you only represented actors.'

'I do, unfortunately. I should only be so lucky as to represent this guy.' She broke the muffin in half and smiled. 'This is, well, a favour, you might say. Jerry Crawford asked me to take a look at the guy.'

'I don't understand, Claire. Is this guy a friend of Jerry's or what?'

Claire's glance skidded away from Shannon's. 'I guess you'd call him an acquaintance,' she said in a muffled voice, brushing crumbs from her ample lap.

Shannon cocked her head to the side. 'I must be missing something. You mean we came all the way out here to watch somebody Jerry Crawford hardly knows play the piano?'

Claire shifted uneasily. 'He doesn't play the piano. He...'

'Are you ladies ready to order?'

'We certainly are,' Claire said emphatically. 'I'll have the—let's see—the meat loaf dinner. Soup, please, and mashed potatoes with the meat loaf and—um—some apple pie and ice cream.' She looked across the table at Shannon and grinned. 'Bring my friend a small salad...'

'No dressing,' Shannon warned.

'Right. And a small steak, rare.' Claire handed over their menus and settled back into her seat. 'So,' she said quickly, before Shannon could speak, 'how did things go today?'

'Terrible,' Shannon said with a sigh. 'We taped tomorrow's show—the others taped it, actually. I didn't even have one line. And I told you that Tony and I rehearsed our big scene.' She waited while the waitress served her salad and Claire's soup. 'Crawford didn't like my performance very much,' she said, picking up her fork and toying with the greens before her.

Her agent sipped carefully at a steaming spoonful of soup. 'Are you sure? I thought he said that you and Tony weren't giving the characters enough life.'

'It comes to the same thing, doesn't it? I'm an actress. I'm supposed to be able to tune out the cameras and the lights and the crew and concentrate on Tony.' She grinned ruefully. 'I'm even supposed to forget that I'm not Tony's type.'

'Females aren't Tony's type,' Claire laughed.

Shannon nodded. 'Yes, but I've played love scenes before, Claire. I know that you don't have to have something going between you and the actor for the scene to sizzle. I don't know, maybe it's just that this particular scene is tougher than any I've ever done. You know, me in that damned bodysuit, Tony with his bare chest, all that moaning and clutching and rolling around in that stupid bed . . .' She lifted her eyes to the other woman's and shook her head. 'The craziest things keep going through my head while we're playing the scene. Today it was laundry . . .'

'Laundry?'

Shannon nodded. 'Yesterday, it was my Christmas card list. And the day before, it was . . .'

Claire held up her hand and groaned. 'Spare me, will you? Let me keep some of my illusions, at least. Next thing I know, you'll be telling me that Krystle doesn't really feel anything when Blake makes love to her.'

Claire's look of absolute innocence made Shannon grin. 'OK, you've made your point. The illusion is what counts—I know that, sure. And I thought, at first, Tony and I had created the illusion. But Crawford wants more. He wants...'

'Sparks,' the agent said, sitting back as their main courses were served. 'Tracy and Hepburn. Taylor and Burton. *Body Heat*.' She cut into her meat loaf and grinned at her client. 'He gave me the same speech he gave you.'

'Jerry? Well, at least he's consistent.' Shannon swallowed a small piece of steak and frowned. 'Which reminds me—you still haven't told me why Jerry wants you to see this musician tonight. Does he want your opinion of the guy's performance or something?'

Claire shrugged her shoulders. 'Or something. Listen, tell me about this visit you people had today from Cade Morgan. I hear it was really something.'

The agent's voice was casual, but there was a glint in her eyes that made Shannon uncomfortable. She must know what had happened, Shannon thought unhappily. She had to. After all, Claire had come on the set only an hour after the whole awful scene. And Shannon had violated one of her agent's cardinal rules. 'Don't draw negative attention to yourself,' she always said, and that was exactly what Shannon had done, in front of her director, the cast and the entire crew.

Confess and get it over with, Shannon told herself. It could be worse. At least she was still employed.

'Look, I don't know what you heard,' she said quickly. 'I admit, it was a bit sticky for a while...'

Claire grinned. 'Sticky? That's not quite the way it was described to me.'

'All right, I behaved like a jerk. But the man infuriated me, Claire.' Shannon's fork clattered against the plate and she leaned across the table. 'Picture this,' she said, her voice an irritated hiss. 'I rehearsed my fourth scene with Rima the Prima...'

'Careful. Some day, you're going to slip and call her that to her face,' Claire said with a giggle.

'Four scenes,' Shannon repeated through gritted teeth, 'and at least that many rehearsals, and the woman still looks right through me and calls me "Miss I'm-sorry-I-can't-remember-your name". And then I spent an hour panting in Tony's ear, only to have Crawford tell me he didn't see any sparks, and then Morgan walked in. You can't imagine what went on, Claire. Until that minute, Jerry had been reminding everybody that we had mountains of work to do and no time to do it in, but once Morgan showed up, well, we had all the time in the world. God, but I am sick to death of celebrities...'

'Shannon, dear, I know how you feel about this,' Claire said quickly. 'And you're right. You should have got the part Rima has.'

'I had it, until Rima turned up wanting a "career in the theatre",' Shannon said bitterly. 'My God, the celebrity system at work! A celebrity can become an actor overnight, but all the rest of us have to keep at it for a lifetime.'

'This is a better part for you, Shannon. You know it is. It's a much better showcase for your talent.'

'They've written the role down for her, Claire. She may be a "star", but she can't act. She doesn't have to. Cade Morgan's another one. He...'

'Don't be so quick to write him off, sweetie.'

Shannon's eyebrows rose. 'All I'm saying is that it was so damned typical—there we were, working our tails off, and in walks this... this over-aged rock star...'

'Come on, Shannon, be fair! The man's thirty-five—hardly a candidate for an old-age pension. And he's not a rock star. He plays blues and ballads, and then there's all that classical stuff...'

'He didn't look very classical, not in that motorcycle outfit he was wearing. I guess that was his macho look...'

'The script girl said he looked sexy,' Claire smirked.

'If you like the type,' Shannon said stiffly.

'Who doesn't? Those gorgeous eyes and that marvellous body and that face and that talent...'

'Interesting that you put talent last on the list.'

'You can't deny that he's got talent,' Claire said patiently. 'He went through Dartmouth on scholarship.'

'That's what his publicist says.'

'Shannon, I won't argue with you. Just listen to the man's music...'

'Are you my agent or his? Don't sell the man to me, Claire. You should have seen his entrance today. He acted as if he were the king come to visit his subjects. Everybody was supposed to bow and scrape.'

'Really?' the other woman asked, glancing coyly at Shannon. 'The story I got from Crawford was that the guy came in alone, without any fanfare at all.'

'Well, maybe,' Shannon admitted grudgingly. 'But everybody sure bowed and scraped. You'd have thought he was...I don't know, royalty or something.'

'He is,' the agent laughed. 'American royalty. His concerts sell out as soon as they're announced...'

'As far as I'm concerned, he's an arrogant, overbearing...'

'They said you could hear the sizzle when he kissed you.'

'What he did,' Shannon said quietly, 'was embarrass the hell out of me. The sizzle everybody heard was me, burning with anger. I wanted to slap his face. I don't know why I didn't, now that I think about it. Maybe it was just that he caught me by surprise.'

The agent shrugged her shoulders and placed her knife and fork neatly across her empty plate.

'"He pulled her into his arms as if he were going to devour her"', she said calmly. 'That's a quote from one of the make-up people.'

'A misquote, you mean. He didn't pull me into his arms. Besides, it doesn't matter. It's over.'

'"Padgett sort of collapsed against him as if her legs had turned to jelly at his touch".' Claire sat back while the waitress cleared away their dishes and served her apple pie. Then she leaned across the table and smiled. 'That's a quote from the script girl.'

'The child reads too many romances, Claire. I did not collapse against him. I barely touched him. I . . .'

'"The second they looked at each other, you could almost see the sparks fly. And when Morgan kissed her, everybody in that studio caught his breath. It was a toss-up as to whether Shannon would kill him or drag him into the sack".'

'Not true!' Shannon snapped. 'What damned fool said that?'

'Jerry Crawford,' Claire said sweetly. 'Your director. Boy, this pie is delicious. Want a bite?'

Shannon shook her head. A prickle of suspicion was beginning to dance up her spine. There was something wrong with this entire conversation. In fact, there was something wrong with finding herself in a restaurant in East Meadow, Long Island on a Thursday night in late October. Claire prided herself on never leaving the borough of Manhattan, except when business demanded. It had even been an effort to convince her to pay a visit to the Cape Cod repertory theatre when Shannon had appeared there.

'Claire,' she said softly, 'why are we going to the Nassau Coliseum tonight?'

'I told you, I have to check out somebody.'

'Why am I going, then?'

'You're keeping me company, Shannon. You're going as a favour to me.'

'And you're going as a favour to Crawford,' Shannon said quietly. Claire nodded. 'You still haven't explained that, Claire.'

The agent sighed and pushed her empty plate to the side. 'OK, why not? I mean, I didn't want to say anything to you until I was certain, but . . . It's almost in the bag, I guess, and . . .'

The prickle of suspicion was doing a dance on the nape of her neck. Everybody seemed terribly interested in what had happened between her and Cade Morgan. And suddenly Jerry Crawford wanted something from Claire—that was interesting all by itself, especially since Shannon had never seen the director say more than hello or goodbye to her agent. Until today, she thought suddenly, until today, when Crawford had spirited Claire into a dark corner of the sound stage and spoken to her in low tones for almost ten minutes; until today, when Cade Morgan had shown up and spoken knowledgeably about *All Our Tomorrows* . . .

She took a deep breath. 'Who's performing at the Coliseum, Claire?' she asked in a soft voice. 'Who are we going to see?'

The woman glanced around her and then leaned towards Shannon. 'Cade Morgan,' she whispered dramatically, 'that's who.' She ran her tongue across her lips and her voice dropped even lower. 'Shannon, listen—Crawford's just about signed Morgan for a role in *All Our Tomorrows*. He was going to do a few days' work—you know, a guest shot thing—but then today... He was impressed by what happened between you and Morgan.'

'Impressed?' Shannon asked in incredulous tones. 'By what? I lost my temper . . .'

'Shannon, listen . . .'

' . . . and Morgan made a fool of me.'

'That's not the way other people saw it, Shannon.'

'Never mind what other people saw,' Shannon said impatiently. 'Cade Morgan and I . . .'

'Cade Morgan and you set tongues wagging on a set where people are so blasé they don't react to anything! That's pretty damned impressive.'

'Look, I'm not going to argue about it. It's over and done with. It's . . .'

'Shannon, listen to me. Jerry and the producers had a meeting this afternoon. They're thinking of playing you and Morgan together.'

Shannon's mouth dropped open and she stared at her agent in disbelief. 'You can't be serious,' she finally murmured. 'You mean, Cade Morgan would play opposite me instead of Tony?' Claire smiled and Shannon shook her head. 'That's impossible. That's Tony's part. It's set . . .'

'So they'll unset it. There's time; your storyline doesn't take off until next week. God, this is so exciting!' Claire leaned forward and placed her hand on Shannon's. 'Everybody would be watching, and I do mean *everybody*. Hollywood people, Broadway people, international film people—they'd all see your work and know your name. This could shoot your career into orbit.'

'Claire . . .'

'And, of course, your part would be expanded. You might end up one of *All Our Tomorrows*' featured players, if things go the way Crawford expects.'

Shannon shook her head. 'I don't believe this. Damn it, Claire, this could end up the world's greatest disaster! It has all the makings of it . . .'

'Disaster? Shannon, sweetie, haven't you been listening? Crawford says you and Morgan will be dynamite together. He says he has Morgan half-convinced to take the part. Crawford says . . .'

'Did he say what would happen if Morgan bombs? The man's not an actor. Crawford wants him because he has an enormous following. He . . .'

'Exactly! Think of the Arbitron shares you'd get! Everybody who has a TV set would tune into *Tomorrows . . .*'

Apprehension filled Shannon with cold dread. 'Claire, listen to me,' she said desperately. 'You know what happens each time the camera's on Rima. She's not an actress—everybody in the scene with her has to carry her.'

'You think that's what will happen with Morgan?' Shannon nodded and Claire sighed. 'Well, I guess it's possible,' she said thoughtfully. 'Although Crawford doesn't think so . . .'

'It isn't fair,' Shannon said in a low voice. 'I've worked damned hard for this chance. I've put in eight hard years perfecting my craft—just think of how many good actors have cut their teeth on soaps. If you can make it in daily daytime drama, you can certainly make it in films or prime-time TV. I mean, what are *Dallas* or *Dynasty*, but once a week, night-time soaps with their long-suffering heroines and dreadful villainesses?'

'You don't have to sell me on soaps, sweetie,' Claire said patiently. 'I don't think anybody has to sell Morgan, either. That's why he wants this part of Tony's. I'm sure he's got his eye on bigger and better things.'

Shannon's eyes flashed. 'And what happens to Tony? Does he get dumped?'

Claire sighed. 'That's one of the advantages to all those characters and plotlines. They'll find another part for Tony. Not that they have to—you know how it is in a soap. Nobody's indispensable.'

'If nobody's indispensable, have you thought about what might happen to me if this over-the-hill guitar player doesn't work out?'

Claire patted Shannon's hand. 'Shannon, sweetie, relax. Crawford wouldn't do anything that would jeopardise the ratings. If he wants to use Morgan, he must figure the guy can carry it off. Where is that waitress?' she added, peering around the restaurant. 'I don't want to get to the Coliseum late...'

The few mouthfuls of steak lay like lead shot in Shannon's stomach. 'I can't believe this. The man has no training, no talent, nothing except his name.'

Claire arched one eyebrow. 'Exactly. His name, his gold records, his fans...'

'He probably has all the acting talent of a mannequin, and I'm supposed to make him look good?'

'I don't think that's what Crawford expects, Shannon. He says the guy has natural talent.'

'In bed, maybe,' Shannon snapped, the words tumbling from her mouth before she could censor them.

'So you do know what came across in the studio today,' the agent said with a knowing leer.

'What happened today had nothing to do with sex.' For the space of a heartbeat, Shannon remembered the pressure of Cade Morgan's hand on her neck and the feel of his mouth on hers. 'Nothing at all,' she repeated positively, forcing the fragmented memory aside. 'I insulted the man and he got even. Period. End. Finished. Why can't anybody understand that?'

Claire sighed and signalled for their bill. 'To tell you the truth, that's what I thought, after I heard the story. But Crawford insisted that wasn't the case. So, while you were scrubbing off your make-up, I talked to a few other people.' She cast a sidelong glance at Shannon and smiled guiltily. 'They saw the same thing Crawford saw.'

'Come on, Claire. Take my word for it...'

'Oh, I do, Shannon. I do.' She scanned the bill and then handed the waitress her credit card. 'That's why I wanted to see Cade Morgan perform tonight.' She slipped her jacket on and smiled innocently. 'Look, you know I wouldn't let you make a bad career move. If there aren't any sparks or flames or whatever it is all those jokers think they saw...'

'Of course there aren't!'

'Then I'll be the first to say so. And tomorrow, I'll convince Crawford it'll be better to let Morgan do his guest shot and to let you and Tony have another go at that scene.'

'But if you believe me, why must we see that man perform? He...'

The agent took her credit card from the waitress and tucked it back into her wallet. 'Look, I promised Jerry, OK? What's the big deal?' Claire glanced at her watch and slid from the booth. 'We don't have much time,' she said. 'Morgan's Marauders come on in half an hour.'

Shannon got to her feet and slipped into her jacket. 'Believe me, if his group's anything like him, that's a perfect choice of names,' she said grimly, following Claire out of the crowded restaurant. 'Wait until you see this man, Claire. There's nothing subtle about him.'

Claire buttoned her coat as they stepped into the crisp autumn night. 'Yeah, so I heard,' she said carefully.

'I'm glad to hear you see this my way. At least two of us are still sane.'

The agent nodded her head as they walked to the kerb. 'Don't worry about a thing,' she said. 'We'll watch the Marauders perform and then we'll go backstage and I'll introduce myself to Cade Morgan...'

Shannon came to a dead stop. 'I am not going backstage,' she said firmly. 'I don't want to see the man again.'

'Look, you want me to get this idea out of Crawford's head, don't you?' she asked levelly. 'Well, how do you expect me to do that unless I can tell Crawford there isn't any chemistry between the two of you? Those mythical sparks everybody talked about...'

'They are just that,' Shannon said. 'Mythical. Nothing more.'

Claire shrugged. 'I can't very well tell him that unless I run the whole thing up the flagpole to see how it flies, now can I?' Claire sensed her client's hesitation and she tucked her arm through Shannon's as the light changed. 'Look, stop worrying. Trust me, OK? We'll say hello to Cade Morgan . . .'

'Not me,' Shannon said quickly. 'I'm not saying anything to the man.'

The agent glanced at her and arched her eyebrows. 'Whatever you say, toots. I'll say hello, you'll glare. Fair enough?'

'Yes, I guess so,' Shannon said reluctantly. 'And then tomorrow you'll tell Jerry his idea's no good, right?'

Claire's eyes slid away from Shannon's. 'Of course,' she agreed quickly. 'Isn't that what I said I'd do?'

Shannon took a deep breath. 'Fair enough,' she said briskly. 'We'll suffer through a couple of hours of bad music and then we'll go pay our respects to Cade Morgan.' She smiled tightly. 'Actually, I'm sure he wants no more to do with me than I want to do with him. In fact, we'd better make sure he doesn't know we're in the house until he finishes performing. Otherwise, he might just have me thrown out.'

'Is his music bad?' Claire asked innocently. 'I'm not sure I'm familiar with it.'

Shannon thought of the softly haunting songs and husky voice she'd listened to for years, and shrugged her shoulders.

'Neither am I,' she said, lying so glibly that she never had time to wonder why she had lied in the first place.

CHAPTER THREE

HAD so many people ever been in one place at one time before? Shannon stared at the stage of the Coliseum, as much surprised by the size of the audience as by its intensity. There had been tickets waiting for them at the box office—courtesy of Jerry Crawford, Shannon was certain, although Claire had ignored her when she'd asked who had arranged for them—and they'd been ushered to two seats in the first row, centre stage.

The auditorium was enormous; there were enough people seated in it to make up the population of a small town. The opening act was just leaving the stage as Shannon and Claire settled into their seats. The crowd applauded politely and then the usual rustles and coughs spread through the huge hall.

The crowd was murmuring quietly, but Shannon was aware of an electricity in the air, a subtle tingle that sent a shudder through her. She felt as she sometimes did on a hot August day, watching the sky darken as a thunderstorm swept in. There was that same sense of something powerful and exciting approaching, the same heady mixture of anticipation and caution.

The house lights dimmed. The first, faint melody of an old Marauders' song sighed eerily through the Coliseum and the audience grew silent. Gradually, smoky-blue spotlights winked on, revealing the Marauders—a drummer, a bass player, and a guitarist. Applause thundered through the auditorium, rolling towards the stage like a mighty wave, meeting the song and curling over it until the applause and the music were a palpable force, throbbing with a life of its own.

'Look,' Claire whispered, poking her elbow into Shannon's ribs. 'Morgan's coming.'

The breathlessly delivered message had not been necessary. One of the spots had picked up a figure at the rear of the stage. Shannon's eyes followed its smoky glow and locked on the man standing motionless beneath it. It was Cade, wearing a chambray workshirt rolled up at the sleeves, and a pair of faded jeans. His head was bent towards his guitar as he twisted the tuning pegs. And then he looked up and smiled, and suddenly the crowd was on its feet, the applause a deafening roar from hands held high as it paid homage to a man who had survived musical fads by transcending them.

Cade moved downstage, still smiling at the crowd, and when he reached the microphone, he nodded and held up his hand. 'Thank you,' he said, the husky words barely audible above the applause. 'Thank you,' he repeated, and the audience quieted in expectant silence. He looked around the huge auditorium and a slow grin eased across his face. 'We're happy to see you, too,' he said, and as the applause thundered towards him again, he turned to the bass player and nodded. The crowd sighed as if with one voice, and suddenly the hall was silent. Cade lifted his guitar and his fingers plucked at the strings. A minor chord thrummed in the darkness, a chord so poignant it brought a lump to Shannon's throat, and then Cade's voice whispered through the darkened auditorium, as smoky and blue as the spotlight, as husky and intimate as she remembered it from the studio.

She sank slowly back into her seat, her eyes never leaving the man on stage. He was singing an old song, a ballad she'd heard a thousand times before. But she'd never heard it sung quite this way: his voice caressed the words and re-grouped the phrases until suddenly the song had a passion and a meaning that made it new. Shannon realised she was holding her breath as she listened; perhaps everybody had been doing the same thing, because

the auditorium was absolutely silent until Cade plucked
the last notes from his guitar strings. A sighing sound
whispered through the Coliseum, as if the thousands
gathered there had shared the song's sorrow together, and
then applause shattered the stillness. Claire turned to
Shannon, eyes shining with delight.

'Have you ever seen anything like it?' she whispered.
'He's got this crowed in the palm of his hand.'

But it was more than that, Shannon thought, watching Cade as he acknowledged the crowd's applause. She
had been at concerts before, and always there was the
sense that you were watching someone perform. Not tonight, though. A special bond seemed to exist between
Cade and the audience. They seemed to share both the
music and the pleasure in each other.

'*Sea Lover,*' a voice called, naming one of his earliest
hits, and Cade nodded.

'Great choice,' he responded, and the audience
laughed with delight at the shared joke.

As he struck the opening chords of the song, a smile lit
his face, curving into the shadowed contours of his high
cheekbones. Shannon caught her bottom lip between her
teeth. Surely it was a trick of the light that made him look
the way he did: powerful, yet with a counterpoint of vul-
nerability. There was no other way to describe the easy
masculine grace of his body and the hint of loneliness in
the sensual curve of his mouth. If only she could see
Cade's eyes, she thought suddenly. His eyes would hold
the key to the real man...

It was as if Cade had read her thoughts. He looked
down, straight down to the first row, to the centre of the
row, and her heart thudded crazily. He was smiling at her,
his indigo eyes telling her things she'd wanted to forget,
telling her he remembered her, remembered their kiss,
remembered the feel of her lips under his and the taste of
her against his mouth...

What on earth was wrong with her? She tore her eyes from the figure on stage and looked down at her lap. She felt light-headed: well, it was warm in the Coliseum. And she hadn't eaten much of her supper, and there hadn't been time for lunch or breakfast. She needed a cup of coffee and some fresh air.

He was looking at her again. She could feel his eyes on her, feel the power of his glance...

Her heart was racing. She raised her lashes slowly, half-afraid to find him staring at her, half-afraid to find he wasn't. Yes, his eyes were on her, there was the shadow of a bittersweet smile on his lips and he was singing about... about some woman he'd loved and lost and...

Shannon took a deep breath. I know what you're doing, Cade Morgan, she thought, forcing her eyes to meet his unflinchingly. You want that part in *All Our Tomorrows*, don't you? You don't want a guest shot; you want something more permanent and meatier, and you think I can help you get it. She lifted her chin. You're not an actor, she thought, but you're one hell of a performer. You gave a terrific performance today in the studio, almost as good as the one you're giving right now. But I'm on to you. Can you see into my eyes from up there? I hope you can, because I want you to read what's in them. You may be able to twist this audience around your finger, but I'm not that easy.

She forced her eyes from his and looked down at her lap. There's a message in that, Mr Morgan, she thought, concentrating on her folded hands. I just hope you understand it. No matter what you do, I'm not going to look at you again until this is over. I'm not even going to think about you. I'm going to run through my lines for tomorrow, and then I'll run through them again and again...

Shannon lifted her head. People were on their feet throughout the auditorium, applauding and chanting

Cade's name. She glanced up at the stage and then quickly turned towards Claire.

'Is it over?' she whispered hoarsely.

Her agent pursed her lips. 'Is it over? What kind of question is that? Yes, it's over. Where have you been for the past two hours?'

'Then let's go,' Shannon said, disregarding the question. 'Come on, Claire,' she said, rising from her seat, 'I've had it.'

The agent stumbled to her feet and tugged at Shannon's sleeve. 'We can't leave yet,' she said. 'We have to go backstage, remember?'

'I don't have to. I'll wait outside.'

'Come on, Shannon. You said you'd go with me.' Shannon shook her head and the other woman smiled. 'He knows you're here. I saw him watching you while he was singing.'

'He can't see anything with those lights in his eyes,' Shannon said quickly. 'It's just a performer's trick, looking out at the audience that way.'

Claire shrugged her shoulders. 'There were no lights in his eyes. The man was looking straight at you.' She smiled and one eyebrow arched delicately. 'What's the matter? Are you afraid of being in the same room with him? I saw the way he looked at you.'

'Of course not,' Shannon said crisply. 'I just don't see any purpose to this. I already told you I don't want to work with the man.'

'Then let me tell Jerry Crawford he's got the whole thing wrong. Come on, Shannon. Remember the old saying, "There's nothing to fear but fear itself"?'

I don't need this, Shannon thought as she followed Claire through the crush to the backstage entrance. Cade Morgan, this whole situation—I definitely don't need it. She wanted to tell Claire she'd changed her mind, but the noise of the crowd drowned everything out and then it was too late. They were backstage. Uniformed security guards stopped them every few yards and then wide-shouldered men in turtleneck shirts and tweed jackets replaced the guards, but, in spite of Shannon's hopes, Claire talked her way past each questioner until finally they were standing in front of Cade Morgan's dressing-room door. Shannon fought back a mounting desire to turn and run. Instead, with a mindlessness that embarrassed her when she thought about it later, she ran her fingers through her hair and wondered if she still had any lipstick on. Her pulsebeat drummed in her ears as the door swung open at Claire's knock.

At first, she thought the room was empty. It was half in shadow, and it took a moment for her eyes to adjust to the lack of light. But, of course, it wasn't. He was there, as she had known he would be, standing before a dressing-table, drying his dark hair with a white towel. He was bare-chested: water droplets gleamed in the dark hair curling on his muscular chest and in the shadowy strip that tapered to invisibility beneath his jeans. Shannon flushed and raised her eyes to his face. Yes, it was just as she remembered it, the cheekbones high and angular, the chin square and strong, and the eyes . . . those eyes . . .

'I'm Claire Holden. I hope we aren't disturbing you, Mr Morgan.'

'Miss Holden.' Cade's voice was soft and flat. He smiled politely, but his eyes never left Shannon's face. 'Thank you for coming tonight.'

'Thank you for the tickets.' Claire shrugged her shoulders and made a face as Shannon shot her a steely glance. 'Look, if this is a bad time . . .'

Cade shook his head. 'No, this is fine. Just as long as I had the chance to take a quick shower . . .'

'Well, I just wanted you to know I enjoyed your performance,' Claire said. 'Miss Padgett and I . . .' Her voice faded into the silence of the little room and she looked from Cade to her client. A smile started on her lips and she moved into a shadowed corner.

'It's nice to see you again, Shannon,' Cade said softly, tossing the towel aside. 'Did you enjoy the concert?'

Shannon nodded. Be polite, she thought. You can manage that, can't you? 'I...yes, thank you, it was...it wasn't quite what I'd expected.'

Cade smiled. 'Really? Is that good or bad?'

'It's...it's neither. I just meant it wasn't the way I'd thought it would be.' He was still smiling, waiting for her to say something more, and finally she shrugged her shoulders. 'It was a very polished performance,' she said carefully.

Cade laughed and tossed the towel aside. 'Somehow, you make that sound like a put-down.'

Shannon took a deep breath. 'I didn't come here to quarrel with you, Mr Morgan,' she said carefully. 'I'm here because my agent asked me.'

'I see.' He cocked his head to the side and his smile curved upward. 'I guess that means Jerry and your agent discussed the possibility of our working together, hmm?'

Shannon shook her head. 'Well, yes, but I think...'

He nodded and dug his hands into his back pockets. 'You think it's a lousy idea, right? Well, I've got to admit, I have some doubts...'

Thank goodness, she thought, letting out her breath. 'Good. I'm glad to hear it. I was afraid...'

His eyes darkened. 'Yes, I'll bet you were.'

'The thing is, I've been an actress for a long time and I understand what happened today.'

'Do you?' he asked softly, tossing the towel aside.

Shannon nodded. At least he was listening, she thought. And he'd admitted he had doubts about Crawford's insane scheme. Go on, she told herself. Get to it...

'You see, you came along just after I'd blown a crucial scene. That's why Mr Crawford misinterpreted what he saw—what he thought he saw—happen between us.'

'I see,' he said evenly. 'So it was simply Jerry's error of judgement.'

'Yes,' she said, and then she shook her head. 'No, I don't mean that. What I mean is that I'm a seasoned actress. And Tony's a trained actor...'

'Which I'm not,' Cade said softly.

It was a statement, but it was more than that. There was a challenging tone to his voice, one it was impossible to ignore. Shannon hesitated and then she took a deep breath.

'Claire—my agent—told me you'd thought about taking a guest role on *Tomorrows*,' she said. 'I think that's a great idea. There's so much you could pick up that way.'

A cool smile flickered across his face. 'Don't be so polite, Shannon,' he said, brushing past her and reaching for a cashmere sweater draped across the back of a chair. 'What you mean is, you think I'd be overstepping myself if I took a role on *Tomorrows*.''

'I didn't say that, exactly.'

He pulled the sweater over his head and turned towards her. 'Then what did you say, exactly?' he asked in an empty voice.

His eyes had gone flat, and a coldness suddenly gripped Shannon's spine. She looked at Claire, but her agent was leaning against the wall, arms crossed, gazing upward with a vacant expression. Where are you when I need you, Claire? she thought desperately.

'All I meant was that performing isn't the same as acting. People think it is, but...'

'That's what I told Crawford,' he said softly.

'Did you?' she said eagerly. 'Well, then...'

'He told me to let him be the judge of that.' Cade pulled his sweater down and smiled politely. 'Don't you think that's good advice, Miss Padgett?'

Shannon's cheeks flushed. 'My agent said...' She looked across the room again. Claire had said she'd go back and try to talk Jerry out of this if she thought it was for the best. But that wasn't what she'd intended to do at all, Shannon suddenly realised, staring at her agent's bemused expression. How could she have been so naïve? Claire had just said whatever had to be said to soothe her. The truth was that the agent had brought her here so she could see first-hand what Jerry Crawford had seen, and even if there was nothing to see, she'd pretend there was. Everybody bowed and scraped, Shannon thought bitterly, even the people you thought were your friends. This man standing before her, this man who made her tense with anger, was going to replace Tony. She knew that as surely as she knew the sun would rise tomorrow. Without warning, the afternoon's disastrous love scene flashed into her mind. Dear God, she thought, if she hadn't been able to play it with Tony, how in hell would she manage it with Cade Morgan?

She turned away quickly and reached for the door. 'Thank you for the tickets,' she said with stiff formality. 'It was interesting.'

Cade grasped her wrist as her fingers closed around the doorknob. 'Interesting? Even unfavourable critics come up with better words than that to describe my concerts, Miss Padgett.'

'Someone actually said something unfavourable about the great Cade Morgan?' she said softly, raising her eyes to his. 'I'm shocked.'

Cade's fingers curled more tightly around her wrist. She could feel the heat of his touch burning through her jacket, through her silk blouse to the naked flesh beneath.

'What's your problem, Padgett?' he growled. 'Can't you get through five minutes without insulting me?'

'I was simply being honest,' she said, looking down at his hand on her arm. 'I was . . .' She broke off in midsentence. Suddenly, all she wanted was to escape the stifling confines of the small room. Cade Morgan's presence seemed overwhelming.

'Was what?' he murmured.

'Never mind,' she said. 'I'm not really in a position to judge your music or your performance.'

He drew closer and bent his head towards hers. 'We're not talking about that, Padgett, are we? You just don't like me.'

'That has nothing to do with it,' Shannon said quickly.

A tight smile spread across his mouth, leaving his eyes untouched and cold.

'It has everything to do with it.' He drew her towards him, his eyes riveted to hers.

No, she thought, no... He was going to kiss her again. She could read it in his dark eyes, in the sultry expression on his mouth. This time, she'd slap his face. This time, she'd tell him she didn't like cavemen... But a honeyed weakness was spreading through her, fuelled by the soft, licking flame that was his hand on her wrist.

'Let go of me,' she said, thinking the words as a command, saying them as a plea. 'Please...'

His eyes searched hers for the span of a heartbeat and then he took a deep breath. Carefully, as if he were letting go of something that might turn on him, his hand released hers and he stepped back.

'Look,' he said gruffly, running his hand through his dark hair, 'maybe we got off to a bad start. I didn't mean to insult you this afternoon. I wish you'd just forget all about that kiss.'

Of course, Shannon thought grimly. His hesitant apology, if that's what it was, was all the proof she needed. The decision to hire Cade Morgan had already been made. And the man wasn't a fool; he knew it would be a lot better to have her on his side than not. Well, he could forget that. She'd deliver when she had to—when the lights and the camera were on—and he could be damned when they weren't.

'I've already forgotten it,' she said evenly, as she pulled open the door. 'As I told you earlier, there wasn't that much to remember.'

She turned her back on Cade Morgan and stepped out into the hall. Cade moved towards her and Claire stepped quickly out of the shadowed corner. 'Hey,' she said with artificial good cheer, 'let's take it easy, kids.'

'Miss Holden.' His voice was ice. 'Tell your client I'm going to take that part,' he said as Claire scrambled to the door. 'Tell her she's going to have lots to remember by the time I'm finished with her.'

Claire nodded and closed the door quietly behind her. Shannon was walking quickly down the corridor, her high heels tapping an angry tattoo against the tile surface. It would be like touching a lighted match to a fuse, she thought, hurrying after her client. Dangerous, volatile—but with breathtaking results. And the explosion would make Shannon Padgett a star.

CHAPTER FOUR

THE door to the Theatre Arts Workshop squealed as
Shannon eased it open. Why didn't somebody fix the
stupid thing? she thought as she slipped into the dimly lit,
overheated classroom. Did it always have to sound like an
over-the-hill soprano struggling for a high C? The actor
and actress reading lines in the glare of the lights at the
front of the room were caught in their roles, thank
heavens. They didn't so much as glance in her direction—
but the two people seated nearest the door turned towards her and frowned.

She mouthed an apology, slid along the back wall until she reached an empty seat, and slipped into it quickly.
The wooden chair creaked noisily—why not? she
thought, fighting against an overwhelming desire to kick
it into silence—and a woman slouched in a nearby seat
glared at the intrusion. So much for unobtrusive en-
trances, Shannon thought, barely breathing as she
shrugged her jacket off her shoulders. Maybe she should
have waited in the corridor until break, but she'd missed
so many classes lately that she was afraid to miss
another.

Not that her teacher had complained; Eli encouraged
his students to take any part they could get, even if it in-
terfered with class time. The Theatre Arts Workshop had
been difficult to get into. She'd had to wait two years after her audition before she'd been admitted. But she knew
she'd benefited from the harsh criticism that was part of
the curriculum, and was a better actress for it.

Carefully, she opened the catch on her shoulder-bag.
The snap of the clasp sounded like a crack of lightning

in the silent room. Shannon froze, expecting another furious stare, then breathed a sigh of relief when none came. Her workshop script was in her bag somewhere, tucked behind the *All Our Tomorrows* script Jerry had thrust into her hands as she'd raced out the door a half-hour before.

'I have tomorrow's script,' she'd said impatiently. 'Jerry, forgive me for running, but . . .'

'The script I just gave you is changed—and your agent called. She'll be along in just a few minutes.'

'Thanks for the message, but I can't wait.'

'There are some things in that script that I'd like to go over with you, Shannon.'

'Tomorrow, Jerry. OK? I'll get in early,' she'd pleaded. She had missed her last workshop class; that, and wanting Eli to help her with what she and Tony laughingly called the infamous bedroom scene, had given her the courage to turn the director down. Jerry had given her a funny look and she'd wondered if she'd overstepped her bounds. Then he'd shrugged and waved her away.

'Yeah, sure,' he'd said. 'See you tomorrow.'

There was a sudden murmur in the small classroom. Shannon blinked and looked up from her shoulder-bag.

'Thank you,' Eli was saying in a non-committal voice. 'Next pair, please.'

Another actress settled on to the high stool and smoothed down her skirt with hands that trembled. Eli nodded to her and she launched into her opening speech. Not bad, Shannon thought. Her voice betrayed her nervousness, but she had the feel of the part. But the guy playing Stanley Kowalski was awful. The class shifted restlessly, a sure sign that they would show him no pity at the end of the hour when they criticised the hour's performances. This was the most demanding of audiences. Playing to these impassive faces was enough to make even the toughest soul want to turn tail and run. Once in a great, great while, if everything went well, you could wrench a stir of emotion from the class. It hadn't happened to Shannon yet, but she was sure that when it did—if it did—she'd treasure the moment. Well, she thought, at least she no longer felt intimidated when she read in front of them. Terrified, yes, but not intimidated.

'Stanley's' voice cracked and a murmur ran through the room. The poor soul was blowing his lines. Eli uncoiled his thin figure from the wall he'd been leaning on and cleared his throat.

'This is a pivotal scene, young man. It's one of the only chances we have to glimpse the real Stanley Kowalski. Try it again, please, and with feeling this time. Remember— the writing is spare and you've got to provide the emotion.'

The scene started again and Shannon's thoughts drifted. Funny that Eli should say something like that— Jerry Crawford had made virtually the same speech to her only a couple of hours ago. They'd been taping tomorrow's show and her dialogue had consisted of three lines with a grand total of fifteen words. It had hardly seemed worth while to bother rehearsing something so simple. Jerry had sensed her dissatisfaction or maybe her boredom, she wasn't sure which, but midway through the fourth take he'd smiled at her.

'Just think of the scene as a skeletal structure, Shannon,' he'd said. 'I'm counting on you to flesh it out.'

She didn't think it was true—you could have cut her dialogue from the scene without losing a thing—but it had made her feel better, although she'd wondered almost immediately why he should care how she felt. Claire swore she had a suspicious mind, but it seemed to Shannon that Jerry had been awfully nice to her over the past few days. Maybe he was making up to her for that unpleasant incident with Cade Morgan.

At least all that nonsense about co-starring them had bitten the dust. She had no idea why—it was nice to think it was because she'd objected—but she wasn't that naïve. After all, she was just an unknown actress; Jerry Crawford and the producers of *All Our Tomorrows* could replace her in the time it took a viewer to tune into a competing drama. No matter how good a case Claire might have pleaded in her behalf, they were interested in ratings and how much detergent and toothpaste the viewers were buying, and they would do what had to be done to achieve both those goals.

No, Cade Morgan must have backed out. Maybe his demands were too outrageous, even for the producers of *All Our Tomorrows*. Maybe he'd chickened out at the thought of pretending he could act in front of fifty million fans—whatever, things had gone back to normal on the set. She and Tony hadn't rehearsed the infamous bedroom scene again, but she was sure they'd be running through it tomorrow. After all, they'd be taping it next week. And it didn't really require any complex acting technique. Maybe Eli could help her find some motivation for her character's behaviour.

The door to the classroom squeaked open. Somebody was even later than she had been. At the front of the room, 'Stanley' had just fluffed his lines again. There was a look of pain on Eli's face.

'Excuse me...'

The latecomer was standing over her. Out of the corner of her eye, Shannon saw him motion at the chair on which she'd placed her shoulder-bag. She nodded, took the bag from the chair and put it on the floor beside her.

'Thanks,' the man murmured.

'Shhh,' she whispered.

'Right. Sorry.'

The chair creaked as he settled into it and she frowned. It was bad enough to come in so late; the least he could do was try to keep noise to a minimum. She gave him a sidelong glance, watching as he opened his copy of *Streetcar* and began rustling through the pages of the first act. She thought of telling him they were reading from the second, but before she had the chance, he leaned towards her.

'Er—could you tell me what page they're on? I can't seem to find it.'

'Page forty-four,' she muttered. 'And could you please be a little quieter? I'm trying to...'' Her sentence ended before it had begun, the words drifting into the air as aimlessly as smoke in a summer breeze. That voice, she thought, while her heart thumped into overdrive, that distinctive voice...No, no, it couldn't be. It was impossible.

Shannon took a deep breath and closed her eyes. Easy, she told herself, easy. Lots of men have husky voices. She raised her lashes slowly, glancing down and to the side. Motorcycle boots, she thought, as mounting panic fluttered inside her chest, dusty black motorcycle boots. Her glance moved slowly up the length of blue-denimed leg beside her. Please, she thought, please...He turned towards her and she choked back a moan. 'What are you doing here?'

Cade Morgan shrugged his shoulders. 'I might ask you the same question.'

'Don't play cute with me!' she whispered frantically. 'I asked you a question. What are you doing here?'

He crossed one boot-clad ankle over the other. 'What does it look like?'

'You...you can't just walk in here and sit down. This is a classroom.'

'Really?' He looked around and then nodded. 'Yeah, that's what it is, all right.'

'Mr Morgan, please...'

'Cade,' he said, leaning towards her.

'Mr Morgan, my teacher will be furious at me.'

'Cade,' he repeated. 'Shall I spell that for you, Shannon? Capital C...'

She took a deep breath. Don't antagonise him, she thought desperately. Don't even try to understand why he's doing this to you. Just get rid of him before somebody realises what's happening.

'OK, OK. Look, my teacher...'

'Cade,' he repeated. 'It's an easy name. Just one syllable.'

She ducked her head and bit her lip as a woman in front of them stirred. 'All right, Cade,' she said swiftly. 'Look, my teacher doesn't let us bring visitors to class. He...'

'No problem,' Cade said easily. 'I'll just tell him I'm not here with you.'

'Will you stop being such an ass?' she whispered in fury. 'You can't do this, you know. You...'

The woman seated ahead clucked her tongue in annoyance and swivelled around to face them.

'For God's sake,' she said through tight lips, 'isn't it enough you both came in late? Must you keep interrupting things?'

Shannon's face whitened. 'I'm sorry,' she whispered. 'This wasn't my idea.'

'You should be sorry. You know better, Shannon. As for you,' she added, turning her angry glare on Cade, 'you shouldn't even be here. You...' Shannon winced as a sudden spark of recognition lit the woman's face from within. 'Aren't you—aren't you——' She raised her hand to her mouth. 'You're kidding,' she said slowly. 'Cade Morgan?'

'No,' Shannon babbled, 'he isn't.' Cade glanced at her and chuckled softly. 'I mean...I mean he was just leaving... That's right, isn't it? Weren't you leaving?'

He smiled pleasantly and the woman touched him lightly on the arm. 'You are Cade Morgan, aren't you?'

'What? Cade Morgan? Where?' The man beside her almost scrambled out of his seat as he turned towards Cade. A smile stretched across his face. 'Jeez, it is!' he said. 'I saw you with the Philharmonic last year, Mr Morgan. Great performance.'

An embarrassed half-smile flickered across Cade's face. 'Sorry,' he whispered to Shannon, shrugging his shoulders in apology. 'I didn't mean to... Thank you,' he murmured, extending his hand to the young actor, 'but I really think we ought to pay attention to what's going on up there.'

The actor grinned and nodded, but it was too late. People were turning around and rising from their chairs, peering towards the back of the room, murmuring softly among themselves. The couple at the front of the classroom glanced up from their scripts and then looked at each other questioningly.

Eli's voice was cold as it cut across the increasingly loud whispers that seemed to fill the classroom.

'That's enough,' he said, and the actors playing Stanley and Blanche were silent. 'What's going on here?'

Shannon moaned softly and put her hand to her forehead.

'Oh, God,' she murmured softly. 'How could you do this to me?'

Cade leaned towards her, his voice quick and urgent. 'It isn't what you think. I'm here because...'

'I'll never live this down, never. This will be worse than what happened at the studio. Why are you doing this to me? Why?'

'I'm not doing anything,' he said, putting his hand on her arm. 'I'm trying to tell you. I...'

She flung his restraining hand from her as if it were an insect. Her script fell to the floor unnoticed. 'Eli,' she said breathessly, scrambling to her feet as the figure of her teacher loomed over them, 'I apologise for the disturbance. I know we aren't supposed to bring visitors to class. Believe me, Mr Morgan barged in on his own—I certainly didn't invite him—and then he wouldn't leave. I'm sorry. I don't know why he followed me here...'

The man was looking at her as if she'd lost her mind, Shannon thought, frowning as his eyes slid past her and fastened on Cade.

'Mr Morgan,' he said with a smile, holding out his hand, 'I'm delighted you were able to join us today. You're quite a surprise to the class, as you can see. I'm afraid I neglected to warn them that you might be joining us. I thought I'd wait and see whether you'd show up today or tomorrow.'

Cade grinned as he stood up and shook the teacher's outstretched hand. 'I probably should have called and let you know that I was coming, but I was afraid that if I did, you might tell me you'd changed your mind.'

Shannon's face burned with humiliation. It was worse than she'd thought. He was there by invitation, as Eli's guest. Oh, God, she thought, I'll never live this down!

'I told you, Mr Morgan...'

'Cade, please. Mr Morgan's much too formal.'

Eli smiled. 'Cade, then. I told you the other day, I'm delighted to have you join the class. I'm sure you'll be an interesting addition.'

No, Shannon thought desperately, no, no, no... She watched as Cade returned Eli's smile with a polite smile of his own.

'I'm grateful to you for taking me on,' he said pleasantly. 'And now I'd be obliged if everybody would just forget I'm here.' The class laughed and Cade grinned. 'Believe me, when you people see me act for the first time, you'll wish I wasn't,' he said, and they laughed again.

The teacher smiled. 'We've had several well known people in our classes in the past. I promise, we'll treat you the same as we treat everybody else once we get back to work. Which is exactly what we'd better do,' he added briskly. 'Cade, we're working on *Streetcar*. I believe I mentioned that when we spoke the other day.'

'Yes, you did. I'm familiar with the play.'

'Well, then, why don't you follow along? Get the feel of things.'

Cade nodded and took his seat again, waiting until things had settled back to normal before he looked at Shannon. She was staring down at the floor, and he took a deep breath and leaned towards her.

'I'm sorry,' he whispered. 'I tried to tell you.'

She waved her hand and shook her head, afraid of how her voice would sound if she tried to speak.

'It's not my fault you jumped to the wrong conclusion,' he insisted. 'Will you look at me, damn it?'

'Just get away from me.'

'Shannon, please...'

'Mr Morgan...'

'Can't you call me Cade?'

'I know what I'd like to call you,' she said, the words exploding from her with fury. 'I know what you deserve to be called. You egotistical bastard!'

Was that loud, cracked voice hers? she thought in horror. Yes, it had to be, because there wasn't another sound in the room. And every eye was on her, including her teacher's.

'Sorry,' she said, closing her eyes as she heard herself. The word had come out sounding as if she were being strangled. She cleared her throat and tried again. 'Sorry,' she repeated, this time in tones that approximated the normal range of the human voice. Shannon forced a smile to her lips; it was almost physically painful to maintain it for the next couple of minutes, but finally people looked away and, after what seemed hours, everybody's attention was back on the actors reading their scene at the front of the room. She took a deep breath and then reached down to retrieve her script.

'I'll get that,' Cade whispered, bending at the same instant. His hand accidentally brushed hers and she pulled back, startled at the sudden heat that enveloped her at the contact.

'I don't need your help,' she spat out.'

'Come on, Shannon, I said I was sorry.'

'Sorry? Sorry? You could walk on burning coals and I wouldn't accept your apology. I . . .'

The girl in front of them turned and stared at them and Shannon bit her lip.

'I'm sorry,' she murmured and the girl nodded and looked away.

Cade shook his head in disbelief. 'Terrific. When you say that word, you expect people to accept it as an apology. When I say it, you just get angrier. Maybe you'd like to explain that to me.'

'Look, just let me be, will you? You managed to make a fool of me again . . .'

'I had nothing to do with making a fool of you,' he said, and then he began to laugh softly. 'I didn't mean that the way it came out, Shannon. Really, I didn't even know you were in this class.'

'I bet.'

'It's the truth. I panicked when Crawford gave me a script and told me you and I would be starting rehearsals tomorrow . . . Now what? My God, woman, must you always look at me as if you wanted to murder me?'

'Crawford said what?' Shannon gasped. 'You and I . . . ?'

'Yeah,' Cade said slowly. 'Didn't anybody tell you?'

Shannon shook her head. 'Nobody said a word.'

'Damn! He said your agent spoke to you about it.'

She shook her head again. 'Why should she?' she asked in a harsh whisper. 'My opinion isn't worth anything.'

'Look, it's worth something to me. I . . .'

The teacher cleared his throat loudly. 'We don't engage in personal chitchat here, Cade,' he said, peering at them over his reading-glasses.

It pleased Shannon no end to see a crimson blush spread across Cade's face.

'Er—sorry about that,' he said quickly. 'I—er—I was asking Miss Padgett—Shannon—what page we were on.'

The teacher nodded. 'Page forty-nine,' he said. 'Look, Cade, why don't you come up here and try a few lines for us?'

A murmur ran through the classroom and Shannon smiled as Cade's blush deepened. The game's up, Mr Morgan, she thought. Your name and your fame got you into this class; well, now it's time to ante up or fold your hand.

'Er—I'm not really ready...'

'No one is ever really ready the first time, Cade. But we've got to start somewhere, and you did say you needed to make rapid progress.'

Shannon glanced at Cade out of the corner of her eye. The rush of colour had faded from his face, to be replaced by a pale mask. She could see a muscle knotting in his jaw. He turned suddenly, his indigo eyes locking with hers, and her smile faltered. There was fear in his gaze but there was something more—a question, perhaps? She turned away sharply and after a second, she heard him draw a deep breath.

'What the hell,' he murmured softly, and then he got to his feet. 'I need more than rapid progress,' he said aloud. 'I need to be an Olivier by tomorrow, Eli. Maybe the play we should be studying is *The Miracle Worker*.'

The class laughed politely as he threaded his way to the front of the room. Cade shook hands with the actor who had been playing the scene and then straddled the stool the man vacated. The actress seated opposite him smiled, only the rose overlay on her pale cheeks hinting at the fact that she was excited at the prospect of doing this scene with Cade Morgan.

'You said you were familiar with *Streetcar,* didn't you?'

Cade cleared his throat and looked up at Eli. 'Right. Actually, I know it pretty well. I had the Kowalski role in my senior year in high school.'

Shannon laughed softly. Cade looked up, his eyes narrowing as they searched the small room. She looked down as his glance met hers. Don't look to me for pity, she thought grimly. Try somebody else, Mr Morgan. When she raised her head, he was staring at his script. She knew what he must be feeling. Even the profession's established names trembled when they read before Eli. Your senior year in high school, hmm? she thought. This ought to be wonderful.

'Are you ready?' Cade asked the girl next to him in a soft voice. She nodded and he took a deep breath. 'Then, let's do it,' he said.

He bent his head while the actress launched into her opening lines, his hands holding the script in a white-knuckled grip. A faint sheen of dampness gleamed under the lock of dark hair that had fallen across his forehead. Shannon sat forward, waiting for his first line, praying that his husky voice would emerge as a the squeak of a frightened mouse.

The girl playing Blanche was good. She'd caught the character's fragility. Cade was watching her as if she held the key to the mysteries of the universe. The self-assured master of the stage had disappeared. In his place was a man with an ashen cast to his skin and a tremor in his fingers.

God, he really was frightened. The pages of the script were vibrating in his hands. Despite herself, Shannon felt a faint stirring of compassion. She could still recall how terrified she'd felt the first time she'd sat up at the front of this room, facing all those impersonal faces, wanting desperately to succeed and yet certain she was going to fail.

It was almost time for Cade's cue. Shannon saw his chest rise as he took a deep breath; then he forced his eyes

from the girl and scanned the room slowly. His glance fell
upon the instructor, but Eli's expression was masked, as
it always was. Shannon knew what he was doing; she'd
done it herself when a part was particularly rough. He
was looking for a friendly face, for someone to connect
with before the scene opened before him like an abyss and
drew him under. Eli won't help you, she thought. He's
the great stone face.

As if he'd heard the message, Cade's gaze moved on,
sliding from face to face, until at last he looked at her.
For a heartbeat, she thought he was going to ignore her,
and then those indigo eyes fastened on hers. There
seemed to be a dozen different messages in their depths:
fear and hope and some kind of plea, and suddenly
something within her thawed.

Don't be so frightened, she wanted to say. You could
have skipped all this, after all. Crawford's already given
you the part. It takes courage to do what you're doing,
Cade. I have to give you that much.

His eyes read hers one last time and then he looked at
the actress opposite him. His first line was delivered
slowly, a bit unsteadily, but his voice gained strength as
he spoke Tennessee Williams' powerful words, and then
a magical thing happened. Suddenly, Cade Morgan was
gone and Stanley Kowalski, crude, almost obscenely
masculine, was there in his place.

Yes, Shannon thought, yes, that's the way. She hitched
forward in her seat. She had seen at least a dozen Stanley Kowalskis during the past few years, at least half of
them right here in this room. *Streetcar* was a play everybody liked to do; it had been done to death, and so had
this part. But Cade's Stanley was not the stereotype she
had seen so many times. There was crudeness there, yes,
but there was also a cruelty, a deliberate awareness of
Blanche's fragility, a determination to sully something
simply because the Stanley Kowalskis of this world have
to destroy whatever they can't understand.

Cade spoke his final lines, the girl playing Blanche responded, and then there was silence. The instructor walked slowly to the centre of the room and cleared his throat.

'Well,' he said finally, pursing his lips. 'That was interesting. Very interesting.'

Cade's smile was tentative. 'That's what I usually say when I've got to tell somebody auditioning for me that I think they're lousy,' he said with a deliberate attempt at lightness.

The teacher smiled. 'I'm afraid you'll find we're much more direct than that. If a performance is poor, we say so.'

'I guess you can't turn me into an Olivier, huh?' Cade asked. Shannon wondered if anyone besides she could hear the anguish under the teasing question.

'No, I don't think you'll ever be a threat to Larry,' the teacher laughed. 'But I must tell you I think we can turn you into a good actor by the end of the semester.'

Cade's pleasure was instant and obvious. 'All right!' he said with a grin, getting to his feet and extending his hand to the instructor. Immediately, the other members of the class were on their feet, crowding around him, until finally he was surrounded.

Only Shannon hung back. She stood in the rear of the room, clutching the doorknob, staring thoughtfully at a Cade Morgan who had magically escaped from the pigeon-hole in which she'd placed him.

CHAPTER FIVE

SHANNON remembered her lines as Alice in Children's Theatre. Curiouser and curiouser, Alice had said, and that was the line that sprang to mind now. She had expected to laugh at Cade's lack of ability. Instead, she had been stunned, even moved. She stared at him a moment longer, and then shook her head. His unexpected talent wasn't the point. The point was that she didn't like him. The point was that she was going to have to play opposite him. Someone should have told her about the casting change... She dug in her shoulder-bag for some coins. The first thing to do was call Claire. Claire could have warned her. And then she'd call Jerry. He could have told her...

Her fingers slowed in their frantic search. OK, they could have. But Cade would still have the part. And she'd still have to make the best of things.

'Shannon...' Cade's voice carried clearly across the room. 'Wait, please.' The babble of voices died away as she turned towards him. 'Please,' he repeated, 'give me five minutes.'

An hour earlier, she'd have cut him down with a sharp look and a sharper tongue. But the memory of the performance she'd just seen lingered. It made her hesitate, and when she turned and looked at him, his eyes held the same searching need that had so transfixed her a short while before. It took an effort of will to tear her eyes from his and shake her head.

'I... I haven't the time,' she said quickly. 'I...I...'

'Please,' he repeated softly.

'I can't,' she insisted. 'I . . . I . . .' She looked past him, the colour rising to her cheeks as she caught sight of her classmates watching them with open curiosity, their heads turning from Cade to her and back again as if they were spectators at a tennis match. Make the best of things, she thought wearily, and she let out a sigh. 'All right,' she said finally, 'I guess I can spare five minutes. I was going to stop for coffee but we can talk out in the hall instead.'

Cade smiled as he walked towards her. 'Are you kidding?' he asked in a husky murmur meant for her ears alone. 'We'd have to assign seats to keep the crowd down. Look, I could use a cup of coffee myself. Why don't we head uptown and I'll buy you some lunch?'

Give an inch, take a mile, she thought as they stepped into the hall. 'No thanks,' she said. 'I never have lunch.'

'OK, just coffee, then. You name the place.'

His body brushed hers lightly at hip and thigh. She felt an electric tingle where he had leaned against her and it made her want to strike out at him.

'All right,' she said, 'there's a place just around the corner that I stop in sometimes. Of course, it isn't the kind of place you're used to, so if you'd rather just go on your way . . .'

He shrugged his shoulders. 'You'd be amazed at the kind of places I'm used to. I'll bet I know every café and truck stop from here to California.' He pulled a pair of dark glasses from his pocket and put them on as they reached the street.

Shannon glanced at him and raised her eyebrows. 'Don't tell me wearing those really keeps people from recognising you.'

'It helps a little,' he said, tucking his hands into the slash pockets of his leather jacket and adjusting his long stride to hers. 'I guess there isn't much to worry about in this neighbourhood. The streets are pretty empty.'

'Yes, this is an industrial area. I should think you're used to creating a stir, though. You've been a celebrity for a long time, haven't you?'

He smiled tightly and shook his head. 'Lord, but I hate that word,' he said. A truck rumbled past them and slowed. The driver leaned out the window, his brow furrowing as he stared at them. 'Just keep walking,' Cade murmured, his long legs moving more quickly. 'New Yorkers are pretty good about things like this. If you don't make eye contact, most of them leave you alone.'

'I thought celebrities were used to . . .'

'Is that what you want? he asked sharply. 'To be a celebrity?'

'Me? I want to be the best actress I can,' she said, looking up at him as if he'd accused her of an immoral act.

'Well, I've spent the past fourteen years trying to be the best musician and composer I can,' he answered, following her into a dingy café. 'If I became a "celebrity" along the way, it wasn't by design.'

'And now you want to be an actor,' Shannon said, deliberately ignoring the censure in his tone.

Cade nodded as they sat down slipped into a small booth. 'It's not something recent. I've wanted to act for a long time. It's just that the time seems right.'

'And Jerry Crawford's willing to accommodate you.'

'Jerry thinks I've got a good chance of making it,' he said carefully. Shannon looked at him, trying to decide if his remark had been a statement or a challenge, but his smiling expression gave nothing away. 'What's good to eat here?' he asked, zipping open his leather jacket. 'I'm starved—I haven't had anything but a cup of coffee all day.'

She thought of her own demanding schedule and managed a polite smile. 'Neither have I. There just wasn't time between my exercise class, rehearsal, and the workshop.' She folded her hands in her lap and looked at him, her grey eyes cool. 'It must be difficult to work late at night. I suppose there's a tendency to go out and unwind afterwards and then sleep in the next morning, but then you don't have to do anything until that evening, do you? I guess it wasn't easy making it to the workshop today. I know you missed half of it, but then, you're probably usually still asleep at this hour of the afternoon.'

'That's not exactly the way my day goes, Shannon,' he said carefully. 'I keep pretty busy.'

'Yes, I forgot about interviews and photo sessions and autographs. That must take a lot of time.'

Cade put both hands flat on the table and leaned towards her. 'Listen,' he said quietly, 'I've got a terrific idea. Why don't you tell me why I rub you the wrong way? Maybe if we get it out in the open, I won't be afraid you'll put a knife in my back every time you see me.'

'Having coffee was your idea, Mr Morgan, not mine.'

'That's true, Miss Padgett. Indulging in fantasy was yours. I gather you'd love to think I spent the night in an orgy of wine, women, and song, and the day between satin sheets, but the truth is I had a couple of beers with the guys in the band and then took a cab back to my hotel. At least I was lucky last night—it was our last concert for a while, but that doesn't mean I didn't have to supervise loading the sound equipment...' He broke off as the counterman loomed over them, two greasy menus in his hands. 'Coffee and a piece of apple pie.'

'Just coffee for me, please,' Shannon said. She waited until the man had moved away and then she looked at Cade. 'Look, Mr Morgan, what you do with your day is your business...' She paused while the counterman slapped two heavy mugs of coffee and a slab of gelatinous-looking pie on to the tabletop and then she leaned towards Cade again. 'You can sleep all day or take classes in nuclear physics or transcendental meditation for all I care...'

'I got to bed around two and I was up at six—we had a seven o'clock rehearsal this morning for a new album we're cutting. We'd still be at it, except we ran out of studio time.' He forked a small bite of pie into his mouth and chewed steadily.

'I'm sure you work hard,' she said carefully. 'But . . .'

'But I'm still sub-human, hmm? Look, I'm sorry you had to find out I'd taken what's his name, Tony's part. Jerry was supposed to tell you or your agent. I know it was a shock . . .'

'I don't want to talk about it.'

'But I do. Hell, we're going to be working together, Shannon. We should get all this sorted out.'

'There's nothing to sort out,' she said, trying to sound more polite than she felt. 'You wanted the part and you got it.'

'You make it sound as if I got it by royal edict,' Cade said carefully. 'It wasn't my idea—it was Jerry's. In fact, I told him I had reservations. But he thinks I can handle it. He thinks . . .'

'Look,' she said quickly, leaning towards him, 'let's stop playing games. Crawford thinks you'll be a better drawing-card than Tony. That's why he signed you. It's that simple.'

'There's more to it than that, and you know it,' Cade said, putting down his fork and shoving the plate aside. 'And Tony hasn't been dumped—they wrote him in elsewhere. Well, doesn't that please you?' he asked after a pause. 'I thought it would. I mean, if you and he are involved . . .'

It was impossible not to smile at the thought. 'Tony and . . . ? God, no.'

'No, I didn't think so. If the guy meant something special to you, you'd have got that scene right.'

Shannon's eyes narrowed. 'What, pray tell, does that mean?' she asked in a softly ominous voice.

'Now who's playing games? You know what it means. Crawford says you played the scene flat. Hell, if it hadn't been for that, he wouldn't have wanted me.'

'Yes, I know,' she asked sweetly. 'I was present at your audition, remember?' Her eyes flashed darkly and her voice dropped to a terse whisper. 'In fact, you might say I *was* your audition.'

'Listen, are you still angry at me because I kissed you?' Cade shook his head. 'I thought I'd already apologised for that. You were explaining the part—you were so damned condescending—and you wouldn't admit you had it all wrong...'

'I did not. Besides, what would you know about it? Tony was playing opposite me, not you.'

'I told you, I'd read the script. Crawford gave it to me when he asked me to guest star...' He ran his hand through his hair and shook his head. 'I'm still trying to figure that out. I was amazed that he wanted me in the first place...'

'Who are you kidding?' she said before she could stop herself. 'He wanted you because you're Cade Morgan. He didn't care if you were good or bad or indifferent. You know it, I know it—everybody knows it.'

She'd gone too far. She knew it as soon as the torrent of angry words had stopped. Cade's eyes had darkened and locked on hers. His mouth was a thin line as he shook his head and half-rose from the booth.

'I don't have to listen to this,' he growled. 'I thought you and I could reach some sort of agreement, but I see that's impossible. I'll tell Crawford it's not going to work out. There's still time to replace...'

There it was, Shannon thought, her heart thudding into gear. The bastard was going to have her dumped. It was almost a relief to have it in the open.

'Not so fast,' she said, fighting to control her voice. 'I have a contract. My union will support me, Mr Morgan, and...'

Cade slumped down into his seat. 'Crawford was wrong, that's all. It was that damned kiss...'

'It certainly was,' she said angrily. 'I'm glad you admit it. It was so meaningless—but nobody wanted to hear that. You took me by surprise, for starters. I didn't have time to prepare.'

'You don't prepare for passion, Padgett. It's not like going to the dentist, for God's sake!'

'We're not talking about passion,' she said. 'We're talking about acting. I should have had time to get into character. I...'

Cade's eyebrows rose. 'What the hell did getting into character have to do with that kiss? You're a woman and I'm a man. Don't you know that?'

'Of course I know that!' she snapped. 'That's just the point. If you knew anything about acting, you'd understand.'

'I understand, Padgett. I kissed you...'

'God, you're insufferable! Of course you kissed me! That's what messed everything up in the first place. Don't you get it? You kissed Shannon Padgett, not the character I play in *All Our Tomorrows*. And it was Shannon Padgett who responded, not her. That's why there were sparks, or chemistry, or whatever it was that...'

Her eyes widened with shock, and the angry words caught in her throat. No, she thought, no—please, tell me I didn't say that—but a quick look at Cade's face told her she had, indeed, said that she hadn't even let herself acknowledge until this second. He looked like a cat who'd been served a dish of bird pudding.

'So,' he said softly, 'Crawford was right.'

'No, no he wasn't. I didn't mean it the way it sounded.'

His eyes darkened and a crooked smile tugged at his mouth. 'It's too late, Padgett. I heard every word. Something happened when I kissed you.'

Shannon shook her head. 'That's not true,' she insisted. Her throat was dry and she could hear her heart pounding in a crazy rhythm. All she wanted to do was look away from him, but his eyes were suddenly deep pools drawing her under.

'Don't lie to me,' he said softly.

She swallowed drily. 'Look, what's the point of arguing about it? You just said you were going to have Crawford replace me. Maybe it's for the best. Maybe I won't even fight it . . .'

Cade looked at her as if she'd lost her mind. 'I never said that. What I said was it wasn't too late for him to replace *me*. I'll do the guest walk-on I originally signed for, and you and Tony or whoever can . . .' An expression of such surprise and relief spread across her face that Cade stared at her in amazement. 'Jesus, did you really think I'd try to muscle you out?'

She nodded her head. 'Yes,' she said softly. 'It happens all the time. Just last week, Rima Dalton took away my best scene. She had them rewrite it for her. And once in summer stock at Provincetown . . .'

Cade leaned across the table and touched her hand. 'You really weren't thinking very clearly, Padgett. Crawford wouldn't ditch you. Don't forget, he only decided to change my part after he saw us together.' She raised her head sharply and he smiled. 'That's just a statement of fact. I've already said I was sorry. And I really didn't mean to embarrass you—it was just that you made me angry as hell.'

'Of course you wanted to embarrass me,' she said. 'You wanted to get even.'

'No, I . . .' Cade sighed and then he nodded agreement. 'OK, maybe. But only after you'd made me feel even more unsure of myself than I already felt.'

'Come on, Mr Morgan. You, insecure? I saw you perform in front of God knows how many people. You had them eating out of the palm of your hand.'

'I break out in a nervous sweat before every performance,' Cade said, flashing her a quick, almost embarrassed smile. 'Besides, all I could think of that day on the
Tomorrows set was that I was surrounded by real actors,
not amateurs like me.' That same vulnerable look that
seemed to reach directly into her soul was back in his indigo eyes. 'I don't know why I let Jerry talk me into
thinking I could act. He insisted it would be OK, that you
and I would be—that we'd make a good team. But I'm no
actor. I'm just a musician.'

Shannon took a deep breath. 'You did a good job with
that reading in the workshop,' she said quietly.

His eyes lit with pleasure. 'Yeah, that seemed to go
pretty well, didn't it? But a fast reading in class isn't the
same as doing a four-month stint in front of a TV camera.'

'Four months?' she said slowly. 'But they told me I
would be killed off in another couple of weeks.'

'Didn't Jerry tell you a damned thing? They rewrote
the script and they figure they ought to get at least four
months out of us.' He glanced at her and then looked
down at the table. 'Of course, that was only because we
were going to be playing opposite each other.'

'Four months,' Shannon repeated in a soft, wistful
voice. 'I never had an acting job that lasted that long.'

Cade cleared his throat. 'Well, of course, that won't
happen now, will it?' He smiled apologetically. 'I mean,
I'm going to tell Jerry that I'm not taking the part.'

'Yes, but . . .'

'Besides, even if I were—even if you and I got along—
you wouldn't want to see your part enlarged just because I'm a "star".' Laughter glistened in his dark eyes
but his expression was grave. 'You wouldn't want to take
advantage of something like that, would you, Padgett?
So what if this would be your chance at the longest-
running, meatiest part you've ever had? So what if you'd

get exposure on a national market? So what if they have
to raise your salary because you've got a bigger role?'

'So what if I could pay my rent on time for a change?'
She put her elbows on the table and propped her chin in
her hands. 'I could learn to live with it, I guess,' she said
softly.

'And me? Could you live with me that long?' He
grinned and leaned back in the booth. 'That's just a figure of speech, of course. What I meant was, could you
play opposite me that long without feeling you'd
compromised all your principles?'

A flush rose to her cheeks. 'Don't make me sound
so...so pompous, Mr Morgan. I admit, I resented you
at first...'

'At first,' he said, nodding.

'I suppose it's fair to admit that what you do onstage
is a kind of acting. I mean, you're not yourself up there,
are you?'

He laughed and shook his head. 'No, not by a long
shot. The real me is always sitting out in the audience
somewhere, wondering what the hell the other me is
doing onstage.' He lifted his coffee mug to his lips and
sipped at the cold coffee. 'It'll be even worse if I take the
Tomorrows role. Crawford wanted us to start rehearsals
Monday and tape later in the week. I have this night-
mare that ends with him telling me to get off the set and
make room for a real actor.'

Shannon looked at him and smiled. 'Don't push your
luck,' she said in a soft voice. 'I already told you that
workshop scene was pretty good. One compliment a day
is about the best I ever manage.'

'Then you're over your allotment,' Cade said with a
wicked grin. 'I seem to remember you said something
complimentary about my kiss.' Her cheeks turned a pale
pink and he touched her hand gently. 'Sorry about that,
Padgett. I just couldn't resist. Anyway, you're right, I

was fishing for another compliment. I was scared to death when Eli asked me to read.'

'Were you, now?' she asked softly, remembering the look of terror in his eyes. 'But you were a convincing Stanley, anyway.'

'Well, thanks for that. But I know *Streetcar*. *All Our Tomorrows* is another thing. I keep looking through that scene where we meet . . .'

'Well,' she said lightly, 'I'm glad Jerry's given one of us a script.'

'I really thought he'd told you,' Cade said. 'He promised he would.'

'Is it the cocktail party scene? That was the one Tony and I had been rehearsing.'

'That's the one. I told Jerry it didn't make sense to me. And he said . . . he said I should remember what happened the day we met.' He stared at her for a long moment and then he cleared his throat. 'Look,' he said gruffly, 'if the director thinks we can do it—I mean, what the hell, Padgett, what have we got to lose? I can always go back to travelling from gig to gig, never knowing what town I'm in . . .'

'The glamorous life of a musician, hmm?'

'Yeah, exactly. When this came along, my agent said I'd be a fool not to give it a shot. I've wanted to try my hand at acting—there just never seemed the time for it. You've got to keep cranking out the music and the records if you want to stay on top.'

'And now?'

Cade shrugged. 'And now, I figure I've been around long enough to take the chance.' He looked up at her and grinned. 'If I make a fool of myself, I'll survive.'

Shannon took a deep breath. 'Would you really give up the part because of me?'

He grinned lazily. 'Listen, don't make me sound like a martyr. If I do the guest shot instead of this part, I can go back to sleeping nights. No more cold sweats, no more bad dreams...'

'Eli says there's no growth without pain,' she said brightly. 'Cold sweats and bad dreams will make you a better actor, Mr Morgan.'

'Are you suggesting I need improving, Padgett?'

Shannon buttoned her jacket and slid towards the edge of the booth. 'What I'm suggesting is that it's going to be hard to play a love scene with a man who calls me Padgett,' she said, not looking at him as she got to her feet. 'The only person who ever called me that was my physical education teacher in tenth grade.'

A grin creased Cade's face. 'OK, then. Miss Padgett.' He scrambled to his feet and tossed some bills on the table. 'How's that sound?'

She smiled. 'Check and mate,' she said, and then she raised her eyes to his. 'My name is Shannon,' she said, holding her hand out to him.

He took her hand in his and shook it with great formality. 'It's nice to meet you, Shannon. I'm Cade.'

'How do you do, Cade? Thank you for the coffee.'

'You're very welcome.' He smiled into her eyes and her heart thudded crazily again.

'Well——' she began.

'Yes,' he said, and then he suddenly reached out and his fingers closed over the top button on her jacket. 'You've closed it wrong,' he said. 'Let me fix it.'

She drew back as his hand brushed her cheek. The sensation of being brushed by flame was so powerful that she flinched. 'I'll do it,' she stammered. Her fingers trembled on the buttons which seemed to take for ever to re-do. 'I guess I'll see you at work Monday. I've got to run now. I've a dance class in half an hour and I'll just about make it if I grab a cab.'

'Let me give you a lift.'

'I wouldn't dream of taking you out of your way,' she said hurrying out the door and signalling wildly at a passing taxi. It was empty, but the driver ignored her in time-honoured New York tradition. Shannon looked down the one-way street; except for a truck rattling towards them, it was empty.

Cade touched her arm lightly. 'Where is your class?'

'All the way downtown in TriBeCa. Near Canal.'

'Well, then you've got to accept my offer. I'm going to pick up my guitarist. He lives right near there.'

'No, I . . .'

'Shannon, really, it's on my way. Jack lives in SoHo.' He glanced at his wristwatch and took her elbow. 'You're going to miss your class otherwise.'

'I . . . I . . .' Shannon took a deep breath and then she nodded. What was the matter with her, anyway? They were going to be working together in just a few days, playing the most intimate scene she'd ever played in her life, and here she was, uncomfortable at the thought of being in a car with him! 'You're right. Yes, thank you, Cade, I'd appreciate a lift. Is your car nearby?'

He grinned and his hand closed around her arm. 'Yeah, it's in a garage right around the corner.'

'I think I'd better warn you that you're going to get hung up in some terrible traffic.'

'I don't think so,' he said solemnly. 'Why don't you wait here for me? I'll only be a minute.'

She nodded her head and tucked her hands into her pockets, shivering in a sudden chill breeze. She watched him as he walked away from her, his long stride rapidly changing into a trot as he reached the corner. A woman walking by paused and stared after him, then shrugged and hurried on. Had she recognised Cade, Shannon wondered, or had she simply stopped to admire his looks? There was no point in denying that he was terrific-looking—his broad shoulders, that narrow waist, and, of course, those blue eyes set in that rugged face . . .

And he knew he was handsome. That had to be why he wore the tight jeans, the macho motorcycle jacket and boots... What kind of car would he drive? she wondered. A Jag, maybe, or a 'Vette... Or maybe a Lamborghini. Maybe nothing so sporty. He might show up in a chauffeured limousine. She'd seen that time after time in the mid-town streets; men whose faces she knew from movies and magazines and television uncurling themselves from the backs of Lincolns and Caddies, not bothered by the fact that they were dressed as if they should be riding by on Harley-Davidson motorcycles instead of being driven around in luxury. But style and image counted. Actors and agents and publicists all knew that.

There was a deep, thrumming roar behind her. She turned quickly and her mouth dropped open.

'Cade?' she said, staring at him in amazement.

He grinned at her from the back of the largest, blackest motorcycle she'd ever seen.

'How about a lift, lady?'

'Is that... that thing yours?' she asked stupidly.

His grin broadened. 'It sure is. Here, put this on,' he said, handing her a black helmet, a duplicate of the one he was wearing. She stared at it blankly and he touched her hand. 'You'd better tuck all that hair up under it. And put the visor down, too. Like this.'

She watched as he slid the smoke-coloured plastic down over his eyes. 'I... I've never ridden one of these,' she said finally.

'Then it's about time you did,' he said. 'OK, why don't you put your shoulder-bag into that carrier?'

She looked from him to the compartment on the back of the bike. 'No, it's OK, I'll hold it.'

He laughed. 'You'll be too busy holding me.'

'No, I won't, I...' She broke off in confusion. Of course she would, she thought, staring at the menacing-looking machine. How else would she keep from falling off? 'Look, maybe this isn't such a good idea...'

'You don't have to worry,' he said, and she could hear the laughter in his voice. 'I said you'd be holding me, not the other way around. Come on, Shannon. Hop on.'

She hesitated briefly and then she took his outstretched hand and straddled the leather seat behind him. God, she thought, where did everything go? Her hands and her arms and her legs...

'OK? Hang on, now.' He revved the engine and the bike began to move. She put her hands on his waist and kept her back straight so that their bodies were separated by inches, but then the bike began to pick up speed.

'Cade,' she said, but how could he possibly hear her? He was wearing that helmet and the engine's roar drowned out her voice, anyway. And they were moving more and more quickly, heading towards Ninth Avenue and traffic and... 'Cade,' she said again. The bike heeled gracefully as they rounded the corner. 'Oh, lord,' she whispered, and she wrapped her arms tightly around him and closed her eyes. She felt her breasts flatten as they pressed against his back, felt the brush of his thighs against hers as she hung on to him for dear life. His body was hard and alive under her touch; she thought she could almost feel the heat of him through the leather jacket he wore.

Wild laughter bubbled in her throat and she fought it back. And I was worried about being in something as confining as a car with this man, she thought. And then they were flying towards lower Manhattan and she gave herself up to the excitement of the ride and the feel of Cade Morgan in her arms.

CHAPTER SIX

THE unseasonable, early evening chill seeped through the walls of Shannon's apartment, crept through the ill-fitting doors and windows, and seemed to linger like the ghosts of years past in the high-ceilinged rooms. Still, the apartment had an old-fashioned charm and grace which soothed the spirit. The bathroom, the handsomest room of all, had Italian marble fixtures, hand-carved mould-ings, and a huge, claw-footed tub. It was a tub in which you could lie back and let tension drain from your mind and body. The only thing wrong with that idea this even-ing, Shannon thought, shivering as a draught played over her wet shoulders, was that she had forgotten how draughty the bathroom was once the cool nights set in, and how quickly the water, never really hot to begin with, chilled.

She stepped out of the tub and wrapped herself in a terry-cloth bath-sheet. The long soak had eased some of the weariness from her bones. A glass of sherry would take care of the rest. Tossing the towel aside, she slipped into an old flannel robe. What an exhausting few days it had been, she thought, stuffing her feet into a pair of scruffy Mickey Mouse slippers she'd owned since her senior year at college. A week of rehearsing her new part had all but wiped her out—and she had yet to play her first scene with Cade.

She padded through the dark hallway and switched on the kitchen light. Should she scramble some eggs for dinner? That didn't sound very intriguing. Well, she could always heat up the leftover Chinese—what was that stuff?—ah yes, *Moo Goo Gai Pan*. But there were no eggs in the refrigerator and the *Moo Goo Gai Pan* had turned into a bright green science experiment in bacterial growth. Shannon made a face and tossed the container into the bin.

No problem. The market had promised to deliver her groceries some time this evening. She'd have her sherry—just a quarter of a jelly glass full, she thought, pouring herself some—and by then her order would have arrived and she could pop a TV dinner into the oven. She'd bought chicken and salisbury steak—or something. It didn't much matter, when you came down to it. All that frozen stuff tasted the same. And then she'd brew a strong pot of coffee and get down to basics, which meant curling up with tomorrow's script and going through it until she had every word and every stage direction committed to memory. She and Cade had started to run through their first scene, and she'd made a mess of it. She'd blown her first lines so many times that he'd never even got to his.

'You're trying too hard, Shannon,' Jerry had said that afternoon, looping his arm loosely around her shoulders and walking her to a quiet corner of the set. 'Just take it easy, OK?'

'Sure,' she'd said, as if she hadn't been trying to do just that all morning. The scene, an easy one, was set at a cocktail party, and all she had to do was look across the set at Cade and see him for the first time. Meeting her eyes, he was supposed to shoulder his way through the room to her side. 'I'm sorry, but I don't think we've met,' was her line. 'Oh, but we have,' he was to answer, 'you've been in my arms in another lifetime.' But they never got that far. 'Have we met?' she'd asked once. 'I'm sorry, but I don't know you,' she'd said the next time. And once she had simply stood mute, staring past him into the distance. And that had bothered Jerry as much as the fact that she kept forgetting her line.

'You've got to look right at Cade when he reaches you, Shannon,' he'd said. 'I'm going to bring the camera in tight—I want every housewife from here to California to feel what you feel.'

So far, all she'd felt was stupid. She kept wondering how long Jerry's patience would last before he screamed or shouted or wrote her out of the part. When Claire had arrived, unexpectedly, at coffee-break time that afternoon, Shannon had immediately suspected Jerry had sent for her.

'Jerry asked you to come by, didn't he?' she'd asked. 'He called you and said I was making a mess of things.'

Claire shook her head. 'No, of course not. I just happened to be in the neighbourhood.'

'Come on, Claire, you don't really expect me to believe that, do you?'

'Believe what you like,' her agent had answered with a non-commital shrug. 'I'm only responsible for your professional life, not your mental condition. If you want to be paranoid, do it on your own time.'

'You're not going to joke your way out of this, Claire. Did Jerry call you? I know I'm doing badly...'

'He never said that. He just said you seemed...tense,' Claire sighed. 'OK, OK, you got me. Yes, Jerry called. He said you seemed to have some sort of block, so I decided to drop by. What's so unusual about that? You know I have only your best interests at heart.'

Shannon nodded. 'The way you did when you neglected to tell me they'd hired Cade Morgan?'

'Oh, come on! You're not still ticked off about that, are you? You know I was going to tell you about Morgan, but you ran off before I got here.'

'I bet you think I'll believe that story if you repeat it often enough.'

'It's the truth,' Claire insisted, her eyes sliding away from her client. 'Just because I made the mistake of telling you it was a good career move, you're convinced I didn't try and talk Jerry Crawford out of it, but . . .'

'Funny, that's not Jerry's story. He says you were hot for it.'

'Look, Jerry had already made up his mind . . . Anyway, what's the difference? You and Morgan buried the hatchet, didn't you?'

Shannon sighed heavily. 'I'm not having problems with Cade. It's—I don't know, I just have this feeling everybody's watching us all the time . . .'

Claire had rolled her eyes. 'Ach, mine child, I was right. Ve have here a case of galloping paranoia, yah?'

'It's the truth, Claire.'

'And a terrible thing it is, too, my paranoid friend. After all, why should anybody watch an actress act?'

A truck rumbled by in the street below and the living-room windows rattled. Shannon sighed and tilted the jelly glass so the last amber drops of sherry slipped on to her tongue. Claire's gentle teasing had virtually convinced her so that later in the afternoon, when they started rehearsing the scene again, she had felt almost comfortable—until she'd noticed people gathering around the periphery of the set, some of them people she'd never seen before. Hey, she'd wanted to yell, what are you doing? Are you all expecting something special? A bolt of lightning, or . . . or . . .

Of course they were expecting something, she thought, pouring more sherry into her glass. The story about her and Cade and that stupid kiss must have made the rounds everywhere and got blown out of all proportion. Probably half the people who'd heard it were convinced Cade had swept her into his arms and carried her off, while the other half believed God only knew what. Everybody was watching and waiting, waiting and watching. It was enough to make any person edgy as a tightrope walker with a blister.

The harsh buzz of the doorbell made her start. Finally, she thought, setting her glass down on the coffee table, her grocery order had arrived, and not a moment too soon. Her stomach was growling; even frozen whatever was going to taste terrific.

'Just a second!' she called, rattling the chains on the door as she opened them. 'I'd almost given up hope, Mario. What took you so...'

Cade Morgan grinned at her from the open doorway. 'Hi,' he said, thrusting a bottle of red wine into her hands. 'Have I missed dinner?'

'...long?' she finished lamely.

'I'd have been here sooner if I'd known you were waiting.'

Shannon swallowed drily. 'I didn't mean you. I was expecting Mario.'

He grinned again, his eyes sweeping from the tousled curls pinned on the top of her head, to her tattered robe, to the Mickey Mouse feet peeking out from beneath the hem.

'Lucky Mario,' he said.

'Mario is the delivery boy from the market down the street,' she said automatically, pulling the lapels of her robe together. Why am I explaining anything, she thought, and what on earth is Cade Morgan doing here? 'Er—did you want to see me?'

Brilliant question, Padgett. Why else would he be standing outside your door? Get hold of yourself.

Cade nodded. 'I hope you don't mind my dropping in. I was in the neighbourhood...'

One dark eyebrow arched upward. 'You're the second person who's used that line today, and I didn't believe it then, either.'

'Look, I was out walking...'

'Walking? In this neighbourhood? Nobody walks here after dark unless they have a Dobermann pinscher with them, and a black belt in karate.' She peered past him and her eyebrow arched upward again. 'And I don't see any four-footed friend by your side.'

'OK, I confess,' he said, putting his hand to his chest. 'I was just sitting around my hotel room, bored to tears, and I decided it was time for some exercise, so I said to myself, Morgan, I said, where in this city can you work up your pulse rate just by outrunning the muggers . . .'

'All right, I admit, it isn't quite that bad . . .'

'And then tone up your muscles by jogging a dozen flights of stairs . . .'

'It's only five . . .'

'And end up standing in a doorway, verging on cardiac collapse, desperate for a drink of the wine you've brought—a vintage year, *madame,* not that you care, apparently—while a beautiful woman wearing Mickey Mouse on her feet tells you she'd rather you were a delivery boy named Marlo . . .'

A smile pulled at the corners of Shannon's mouth. 'Mario,' she said. 'His name is Mario. And you're not verging on anything. You're not even breathing hard.'

Cade's eyes flickered over her and he grinned. 'I can't imagine why not,' he said. 'That sexy outfit you're wearing is enough to drive a man insane with lust.'

She chuckled softly. 'Mario likes it,' she said, and then she opened the door and stepped back. 'OK, you can come in for a minute. How can I turn away a man with such discriminating taste? I just hope none of my neighbours saw you. They'll beat my door down.'

Cade shook his head as the door closed behind him. 'Nobody saw me, except for the group of kids sitting on the stoop downstairs. They were so busy looking at my bike that they didn't pay much attention to me.'

'Your bike? But they'll . . .'

'They'll guard it with their lives,' he laughed, unzipping his jacket. 'I paid them ten bucks to watch over it and I promised them another ten if it's still in one piece later.' There was a moment's silence and then Cade's eyes swept over her again, lingering on the curve of her hip and the swell of her breast, clearly outlined beneath the somewhat damp flannel robe. 'Did I get you out of the bath or something?'

'No, no, I . . .' She swallowed hard, suddenly aware of the fact that she was naked under the worn, thin fabric of her robe. 'I was just going to get dressed,' she lied, backing towards the bedroom. 'Why don't you open that wine while I . . .'

A slow smile spread over his face. 'Yeah,' he said, turning away from her. 'That's a good idea. Do you have a corkscrew anywhere?'

'There should be one on the kitchen counter,' she called from behind the bedroom door. Her heart was tripping into overdrive. Well, anybody's would, she told herself, stripping off her robe with trembling hands. After all, the man had taken her by surprise. She pulled open the wardrobe door and stared at the clothing in it, but her mind was blank. Jeans, she thought finally, and a sweatshirt and my sneakers. At least, that didn't take any planning. OK, she thought, OK, that's it . . .

Not quite, she thought with a groan, catching a glimpse of herself in the mirror. Her hair was a disaster. She yanked out the clips that held it up and it tumbled around her shoulders. Quickly, she combed through the tangles and fluffed the dark curls around her face. The ends were damp, but it would do. Do for what? she thought, but the question was more than she wanted to deal with just then. Right, Padgett, she thought, taking a last deep breath. You're on.

Cade was standing at the window, gazing down at the street. He turned towards her and smiled.

'I should have asked you to keep the slippers on,' he said, holding a glass out to her. 'Mickey is one of my favourite people.'

Cade Morgan, famous musician, she thought, drinking what is probably a very expensive wine out of my very best jelly glass. She bit back a nervous giggle and smiled at him.

'Thanks. I'd offer you some cheese and crackers, but I'm afraid the cupboard is bare.'

'Look, you don't have to mince words, Shannon. You must be wondering what I'm doing here.'

'Well, yes, you could say that.'

He flashed her a quick, boyish grin. 'I don't suppose I could convince you that you'd forgotten you invited me for supper... No, I didn't think so,' he said. 'But it was worth a shot. Would you believe me if I said I'm not exactly sure, myself? I really was just out for a ride—well, worrying and riding. I was going over that damned scene we rehearsed today and...'

'The scene we didn't rehearse, you mean,' she said, sinking down on to the couch. 'Look, I'm really sorry about that. I told Jerry I'd get it right tomorrow.'

'What a hell of a day it was,' he said, sinking down on the couch and stretching his legs out in front of him. 'The rehearsals, the taping, the make-up, the costumes... Is it always like that?'

Shannon smiled. 'Sometimes it's worse. It's not easy to do a one-hour show, five days a week, and juggle so many storylines and characters.' She crossed the room and sat in a wing chair opposite him, tucking her legs up beneath her. 'But daytime drama must be easier than doing concerts. At least you stay in one place.'

Cade sighed. 'That's the truth. I haven't done that since I was at school.'

Shannon sipped her wine and then rested the glass on her leg. 'Princeton, right?' He looked at her in surprise and she blushed. 'Well, your life story isn't exactly a secret,' she said. 'Every magazine on the stands has done something about you at one time or another.'

'And hardly any of it the truth,' he said.

'Is Princeton the truth?'

He grinned. 'Yeah. Hard to believe, right? Me, a music major at a place like that . . .'

'Easy to belive, after seeing you play with the Marauders last week.' She blushed again and he smiled.

'That's nice,' he said softly.

'What?'

'That blush. I didn't think women did that any more.'

To her horror, she felt the colour in her cheeks heightening. 'An inherited trait,' she said lightly. 'All the women in my family blush. My mother, my aunts, my cousins . . .'

Cade laughed. 'And where are these hoardes of blushing females? How come they haven't America by storm?'

She rose and padded across the room. 'They're back home in Kansas,' she said, refilling her glass.

'Waiting for you to win an Emmy or a Tony or an Oscar?'

'Waiting for me to give all this up as a bad idea and come home,' she laughed. 'I think they've heard too many stories about starving in the name of art. Would you like more wine?'

Cade nodded and held his glass out to her. 'It's true, though. For every musician making a living, there must be fifty who aren't.'

'Is that why you didn't stay with classical guitar?'

'The money?' he asked and she nodded. 'No, it wasn't that. Well, it was, at the beginning . . .' He grinned self-consciously. 'Are you sure you want to hear this?'

'If you want to tell me.'

He sighed and leaned back against the couch. 'I was a scholarship student, which meant I was broke most of the time. I started playing at clubs near school on weekends—my own stuff, mostly—and after a while I realised that I'd always love classical guitar but, I don't know, there's a reality to other music . . .' He laughed softly. 'How's that sound? Pompous? Pretentious? Trite?'

'Honest,' Shannon answered, smiling at him. 'I just wish there were as much reality in the soaps. But then, who would watch them?'

'Yeah,' Cade said with a sigh, 'I noticed. My character—Johnny Wolff—seems awfully one-dimensional. Nobody can be that wicked.'

'Alana Dunbar can,' Shannon said. 'My girl's a cold, calculating shark. In fact, the first time she really thaws is...is when she meets Johnny.'

'Ah yes, back to today's horror show. I don't know if I'll ever get that scene right. I told Jerry...'

'It wasn't your fault, Cade. I never even gave you a chance to say your lines, but tomorrow, I...'

'Does the entire population of Manhattan always stand around watching a rehearsal? I'm not sure I want a chance to get to my lines tomorrow if it means every adult this side of the Continental Divide will be leering at us.'

She looked at him in surprise. 'You noticed?'

Cade laughed. 'I've seen fewer people at one of my concerts. I kept expecting someone to sell popcorn.'

Shannon let her breath out and slumped back against in the chair. 'So much for paranoia,' she muttered.

'I don't understand.'

'I told Claire—my agent—virtually the same thing and she said I was crazy. But I knew I wasn't. I've never seen an audience like that at a rehearsal.'

'Well, that's because it wasn't an audience. It was a bunch of gawking idiots, waiting to see me make an ass of myself.'

'What? Don't be silly, Cade. That wasn't it at all. Those people...'

He sprang to his feet and stalked across the room. 'Come on, Shannon, we both know that those people think of me as an intruder.'

'An intruder?'

He shrugged his shoulders and jammed his hands into the back pockets of his jeans. 'You know what I mean,' he growled. 'All those actors and technicians, watching me, knowing I got a chance some of them would give their right arms for.' He took a deep breath and swung around to face her. 'I don't blame them for wanting to see me mess up. But, damn it, you can't blame me for not wanting to give them the satis...' He broke off in the middle of the sentence and his face darkened. 'I don't think that's funny, Shannon,' he said stiffly. 'Nobody wants to fail, especially not in front of an audience.'

Shannon rose from the chair and walked towards him. 'Cade,' she said gently, 'you don't understand. Those people weren't there to see you fail. They heard about... about what happened the day we met, you see, and about all the things people said about it, and...and...' She took a deep breath. 'They want to see us together,' she said finally. 'They want to see if what they've heard is true.'

He looked at her blankly. 'What they've heard?'

Her eyes narrowed and she stared at him. If he's playing games with me, she thought, if he's putting me on... But Cade was looking at her as if she were speaking another language. My God, she thought, is he so terrified of failing that he thinks the whole world is watching him?

'Sparks, remember?' she said with false brightness. 'They want to see if the room lights up when we play our love scenes.'

'If the room...' His eyes widened. 'Really? Is that what they're waiting for?' She nodded her head and a smile lit his face. 'Damn it, that's terrific!'

'There's nothing terrific about it. I don't want to burst your bubble, Cade, but those people are going to be very disappointed.'

'That's it,' he said, flashing her a quick, uncertain smile. 'Give me a vote of confidence and then snatch it back. I thought you said they weren't waiting to see me fall on my face.'

'My, what an ego we have, Mr Morgan. Didn't you hear me? Those people are watching us, not just you. I'm the one who's supposed to be the pro.' She laughed shakily. 'Hasn't it occurred to you that no matter how well we play that scene, it's not going to be good enough?'

Cade shook his head. 'I don't understand. If you're an experienced actress and if they're not waiting for me to bomb...'

'Damn it, you numbskull, nobody's the least bit interested in us as actors. They want to see us together. That's what I meant when I said it's not going to be good enough. Everybody's expectations are so crazy...' Shannon's words stumbled to a halt was a crooked smile flickered across his face. 'What is it?'

He crossed the room slowly and paused beside her chair. 'I wish to hell I'd known all this before,' he said softly. 'I'd have told you there isn't a thing to worry about.'

'Of course there is. It's as if everybody's forgotten we're acting. They're bound to be disappointed.'

Cade reached down and took the empty glass from her hand. She watched as he set it on the table.

'Let me show you something,' he said, twining his fingers through hers.

'Show me what?' Her voice was wary, but she let him pull her slowly to her feet. 'Cade?'

'Nobody's going to be disappointed,' he said, drawing her towards him. 'Not Jerry, not that crowd of gawkers...'

Her heart thumped erratically and a sudden coppery taste flooded her mouth. 'Cade, don't...'

'Not anybody, Shannon. I guarantee it.'

His eyes were narrow slits of blue darkness and his fingers steel clamps around hers. She shook her head, her body tensing instinctively as the space between them lessened until finally they were only a breath apart.

'Cade, please...'

His hand tangled in the cascade of her hair as he bent his head to hers and her whispered plea was lost against his mouth. For an instant she struggled against him, and then her blood grew thick in her veins. She made a sound that was half moan, half sigh as Cade gathered her against him, crushing her until she felt that she was moulded to him. She leaned into his embrace, burrowing into the hardness of his chest, stretching herself against the hard length of him, as if her legs might collapse under her. His lips teased at hers, urging her to open her mouth to him, urging her to taste and be tasted, and she made soft, inarticulate sounds as she did as he demanded.

He tasted just as he had the first time he'd kissed her, she thought, only now there was the added tang of the wine on his tongue, blending with the savour she remembered as his and his alone. She freed her hand from his and spread it on his chest; the other moved to the nape of his neck. She wanted to feel the heat from his body burning through her palm, through her fingers . . .

A horn blasted in the street below, shattering the stillness that had settled around them. Cade growled at the interruption, but Shannon grasped it as she would a lifeline, pulling free of his embrace and backing away from him. Only his eyes followed her, dark indigo stones set in his face. She could feel the heat of his probing stare spreading over her skin. She tried to speak, but her throat was constricted. What in God's name was happening to her? She, who was always in control, she who was so disciplined . . .

'Why did you do that?' she whispered.

He had a thousand answers; he had no answers. In the end, all he could do was make a half-hearted attempt at lightening the tension that had suddenly filled the room.

'Nobody's going to be disappointed,' he said huskily, reaching out and running his finger across her lips. 'Now you can relax.'

His voice was as warm as his breath. For a fragment of eternity, her eyes closed and she swayed towards him—and then his throaty whisper sorted itself into words she could understand. Of course, she thought, the love scene! The scene won't be good enough, she'd said, and he'd taken her in his arms to prove her wrong. But he'd proved more than that, she thought in sudden panic. He'd proved that he could turn her world upside down each time he touched her. And he knew it—he knew it... The realisation set her pulse pounding.

'I almost forgot the knack you have for getting into your character,' she said in an artificially bright voice. 'I'm glad of that; I work better that way, myself. I guess Eli's really been working you hard to refine that technique, hmm?'

Cade shook his head. 'Listen, Shannon, Eli's got nothing to do with this. I...'

'Oh, I know you did a lot of this on your own. I mean, I remember the day you auditioned. Well, I know you said you weren't, not consciously, but on a subconscious level, you wanted to impress Jerry... Look, I'm not angry about it, Cade. I understand. I'm an actress, after all. I believe in illusion. It's the way I make my living...'

Stop babbling, you fool, she thought fiercely. There's no point in wondering why he affects you this way. What matters is that the two of you are going to be the next Tracy and Hepburn. That love scene is going to sizzle! You're Cade Morgan's ticket to success, and he's yours.

'I think we should have some more wine,' she said, moving past him and reaching for the wine bottle. 'And I'd like to propose a toast. To acting. And to the team of Morgan and Padgett.' She refilled their glasses, hoping he wouldn't notice that her hand was trembling as she held a glass out to him.

'Shannon...'

'Come on, partner. Don't you believe we're gonna knock 'em dead?'

'Of course I do,' Cade said slowly. 'But ...'

The rasping buzz of the doorbell filled her with a sense of relief. 'My groceries, at last,' she said, snatching her shoulder-bag from the table. 'I'll just be a minute.' She opened the door and smiled at Mario. 'I'm so glad to see you,' she whispered, taking the groceries from him. His twelve-year-old face puckered in surprise as she pushed two dollars at him. 'For you,' she said. 'And here's the money for the groceries.' The boy was still staring at her as she closed the door and turned back to Cade. 'How does this sound?' she asked, smiling at him over the top of the bag. 'One frozen diet chicken dinner, one frozen diet salisbury steak, frozen cauliflower, frozen yoghurt sundaes and coffee.'

His eyes moved over her face, pausing when they met hers, and then he smiled.

'Instant coffee, I hope,' he said.

'What else?'

'Sounds perfect,' he said, returning her smile.

'I forgot that I was talking to the king of the road,' she laughed, heading towards the kitchen. 'A man who knows his way around every café in the United States probably thinks frozen foods are home cooking. Well, come on back here and open some boxes. You don't think this is going to be a free ride, do you?'

Cade tossed down the last of his wine and shook his head. 'No,' he said, following after her, 'a free ride's the last thing I'd expect.'

CHAPTER SEVEN

THE bed squeaked ominously as Shannon eased herself down on it. 'It's still making funny noises,' she called into the shadowy darkness surrounding the lighted set. Someone chuckled in reply. Shannon could feel her cheeks reddening, but she kept her chin up and her eyes never wavered from the spot where she knew Jerry Crawford was standing. 'I just don't want to waste any more time,' she added carefully. 'Otherwise, I wouldn't mention it . . .'

'It's OK, Shannon,' Crawford said. 'It won't collapse again.' There was another giggle and then a soft laugh. 'Quiet,' Jerry barked, 'or I'll clear the damned set. We've got work to do.'

Please, Shannon thought, please, let something go right. Maybe some day she'd be able to look back at today and laugh—from the start, things had gone like a skit from *Monty Python's Flying Circus*—but right now she felt closer to tears than laughter. At nine o'clock, the mike boom had collapsed for no apparent reason. They'd no sooner fixed it than Rima the Prima had gasped and dropped to her knees. For a few panicked seconds, everybody had thought she'd had a heart attack. But it turned out that Rima had lost a contact lens, and the cast and crew had spent twenty minutes crawling around on the floor, looking for the darned thing, which, of course, they never found. What they did find was that the famous Rima the Prima's emerald eyes weren't emerald at all. Without the artificial colour added by the contacts, they were a pale, near-sighted hazel.

And then it had been time to rehearse the scene and, as the time had grown near for the first run-through, she'd begun to feel the cold touch of panic. Who would be on that bed with Cade Morgan? she'd wondered suddenly. Would it be Shannon Padgett or the character she was playing? Cade's assurance that the scene would sizzle was suddenly not comforting at all. Why hadn't it occurred to her that knowing he could draw such a passionate response from her was dangerous? If she wasn't going to be an actress playing Alana Dunbar, who would she be? Crawford had hated the way she'd played this scene with Tony. No passion, he'd said, but that had been safer than losing control of herself in Cade's arms...

At least they hadn't been in costume for the first rehearsal. If Jerry had told her to change into the flesh-coloured bodysuit, she'd never have been able to walk to that awful bed, much less sit down on it. As it was, she'd moved towards it with all the grace of a badly controlled marionette. She'd managed to say her lines when Cade had materialised before her, but even she knew her delivery had been wooden. And when he'd smiled and begun to walk towards the bed, his eyes and voice caressing her as if they were a man and a woman alone in a real bedroom in a real apartment, panic had exploded deep inside her.

'You're going to feel the planet spin when I touch you.' That was Cade's first line. And she knew it would. But an actress couldn't afford to lose control. She couldn't afford to lose control.

'You're going to feel the planet spin,' he'd said as he had knelt down beside her, and then the damned bed had swayed, groaned, and with a shriek of rending metal collapsed in a heap, tumbling them to the floor in an undignified spill of pillows, sheets and blankets. There had been a second of stunned silence, and then everybody, including Cade, had burst into peals of laughter. Everybody but Shannon. Well, Jerry hadn't laughed, either, but it wasn't because he'd been mortified the way she'd been. It was because he was angry at all the delays. And there were more to come.

'Fix the freaking bed,' Jerry had snarled, stalking off the set. While the grips had hammered and sawed, the make-up man had scurried over and said he'd been asked to make her eyes look darker. Wearily, Shannon had closed her eyes while he applied some new shadow and liner. 'Smashing, darling,' the make-up man had cooed, but by the time the bed was in one piece again and Jerry had waved her back to the set, her eyes were tearing and red.

'It's probably just a little allergic reaction,' she'd assured Jerry while she tissued the make-up off. 'It's nothing...'

'Nothing,' the make-up man had echoed frantically. 'Nothing...' Rushing desperately to her side, he'd tripped over a cable and blew an entire set of lights.

'God give me strength!' Jerry had screamed. 'What next?'

The heating system was what had come next. The radiators suddenly set up a clatter that was loud enough to raise ghosts on Hallowe'en, and then the whole system had died. Within minutes, the huge studio was like a walk-in refrigerator, so that now everybody was standing around in coats and hats.

But there were still small miracles in the world, Shannon thought, shifting cautiously on the bed. Jerry had wanted a dress rehearsal, which meant that if the heat hadn't failed, she'd have been sitting here, staring into the darkness, wearing nothing but a flesh-coloured bodysuit, feeling more naked than a bald man in a hairdressing salon. And she'd be waiting for Cade, waiting for him to make his entrance and move on to the bed beside her, waiting for him to take her into his arms and...

'Shannon?'

A shiver of apprehension ran through her. Jerry's voice was a silken sigh, an ominous portent considering the mood he was in.

'Yes?' she asked in a cautious whisper.

'Is there a problem, Shannon?'

'No, of course not,' she said quickly. 'I'm just waiting.'

'For what? A visit to the dentist?' She cringed at the acid tone of his voice. 'Passion, Miss Padgett, passion! I want to see longing on your face, not resignation. Jesus, is that so much to ask? And where's Make-up, damn it? Haven't you got something you can use to kill the shine on her nose, Make-up? Her nose looks like my mother's freshly waxed floor!'

Shannon cleared her throat. 'I...I asked him to go easy on the powder, Jerry. I was afraid I might have another allergic reaction. You see, sometimes these things are cumulative. Once I couldn't wear make-up for a week, and...'

Crawford threw his arms up in disgust. 'OK,' he roared, 'OK, that's it. Everybody, go home. Go on, get out of here! What is this, a conspiracy? It's bad enough I'm freezing my tail off, working in this barn they call a studio while it collapses around me, without having you tell me that we may have to tape tomorrow's show with you looking like a Vestal Virgin.'

'I'm sure I'll be fine by tomorrow, Jerry. I'll take an antihistamine when I get home...'

'Listen, spare me the details, OK? Just get yourself in shape for an early start. I want you here at six a.m., Miss Padgett. We'll work straight through until late afternoon and then we'll tape the damned thing. Is there an outside chance you manage to turn into an actress by then?'

She swallowed hard and nodded. 'Yes, Mr Crawford. I know I can. I...'

Crawford grimaced. 'I hope so. Otherwise, I'll have to assume I made a mistake in casting you, Miss Padgett. Maybe those sparks were a one-shot. Maybe I'm better off hoping for competency. Maybe I should call casting . . .'

'I'll be fine tomorrow. You'll see. I . . .'

'I damned well don't have any more time to waste. You got that?'

Shannon nodded again, watching in silence as the director tossed his script aside and stalked off the set. Oh, God, she thought, lacing her trembling hands together in her lap, oh, God, he's going to replace me. He's going to fire me. He's . . .

'He's not blaming anything on you, you know. He's just frustrated.'

Her head sprang up at the sound of that familiar, husky whisper. 'Cade?' she murmured.

He stepped out of the shadows and sat down on the bed beside her. 'Stop looking as if Jerry had just handed you your notice. It was just a bad day for everybody. Anyway, I think we'll all feel better when we get this damned scene out of the way.'

'If we ever do,' she said in a mournful whisper. 'Well, I guess I'll see you tomorrow,' she added, getting slowly to her feet.

'You guess? Don't you plan on being here?'

'Sure. But Jerry may decide to replace me before then.'

'Don't be silly, Shannon. He wanted us as a team, remember? You're the reason he signed me for this part. He's just angry.'

'Sure,' she said tonelessly. Suddenly, her eyes widened. 'I wonder if there's time to catch Eli at the workshop.'

'Didn't he say he was going to be in Boston this week with the new Shepherd play? What did you want to do? Read lines with him?'

She shook her head. 'No, I know my lines.'

'Well, then, what's the problem? If you know them...'

A touch of pink rose to her cheeks and she turned away from Cade's puzzled face. 'There's no problem,' she said quickly, snatching up her jacket and starting across the studio. 'I...I just thought...I'll be fine, Cade. Don't worry. I'll spend the night going over the scene and...'

'You know what you need, Padgett? You need to relax. And I know the way to get you unwound.' She tossed him a sharp glance and he chuckled softly. 'For shame,' he murmured, taking her hand in his. 'Whatever are you thinking?'

She tugged her hand free of his. 'Look,' she said wearily. 'I'm exhausted. I don't have the time or the energy for any verbal skirmishes. I'm going home to work on my role.'

'That's a mistake. You need to let go for a while.'

'I know what I need, Cade. I should after all these years.'

'I know, I know—you're the pro and I'm the novice. OK, maybe that's true, but I've been performing more than half my life, Shannon. I know something about stage fright.'

'For God's sake, I haven't got stage fright! I just need to put in some more time with this script.'

'Wrong, Padgett. You need time away from it. Trust me.' He pushed open the door to the street and looked up at the sky as they stepped outside. 'Look at that. You can almost see the sun in spite of the pollution. Wouldn't you like to go somewhere, breathe fresh air, and forget about *All Our Tomorrows* for a while?'

'Sure,' she admitted with a sigh. 'But I can't. I have work to do. Goodbye, Cade. I'll see you tomorrow.'

'All right, all right, you win. I'll ride you home and leave you to your work. Come on, don't look at me like that. You know darned well I can deliver you to your doorstep in half the time it would take to get there any other way.'

Well, he had her there, she thought, eyeing the big Harley parked at the curb. The bike was fast and she knew Cade could manoeuvre it easily through the crowded streets, taking quick advantage of every hole in the traffic. 'All right,' she said finally. 'I guess you're right.'

'I know I am,' he said, handing her a helmet. 'Just trust me, Shannon. I know what I'm doing.'

'Trust me, you said. I know what I'm doing, you said.' Shannon slid from the Harley as it came to a stop. 'Where in God's name are we?' she demanded. 'Damn it, Cade, you . . . you kidnapped me! Why didn't you stop when I asked you to?'

Grinning lazily, Cade eased himself off the bike and pushed his visor up. 'One question at a time, lady. We're at Jones Beach. Don't tell me you've never been here before. It's only thirty-something miles from the city.'

'Spare me the geography lesson, please. Why didn't you stop when I . . .'

'I didn't hear you,' he said with wide-eyed innocence. 'The engine noise must have drowned you out. Besides, you said you wanted to work, didn't you? Well, this is the perfect place.'

'Sure it is. Just you and me and the seagulls. Look, you've had your little joke. Take me back to the city, OK?'

'Where's your spirit of adventure, woman? Just smell that ocean breeze. And wait until you feel the sand between your toes.'

'I want to feel my living-room carpet between my toes, Cade. And I want to smell the coffee brewing in my percolator.'

'What a terrific idea,' he said, taking her hand in his. 'Coffee and cake . . .'

'Cade . . .'

'And the world's greatest chowder. Well, maybe not the greatest, but...'

'Will you listen?'

'You've got a choice, Padgett. Chowder and coffee and a walk on the beach and in an hour I'll take you back to New York and deliver you, safe and sound, at your apartment.'

She looked at him warily. 'Or?'

'No chowder, no coffee, no walk and you can make it back to the city on your own. I know there's not much traffic on this road, but it's only five miles or so to the main road. You can probably hitch a ride once you get there.'

'Kidnapping and now blackmail,' she said in tones as chilled as the salt-laden breeze blowing in from the ocean.

'Not at all, Padgett. Just old fashioned R and R. Rest and recuperation, as we used to say in the army.' Cade tucked her hand inside his, completely ignoring her attempts to pull free. 'Why don't you just relax and enjoy the afternoon?'

'Enjoy being dragged off to some...some posh restaurant that caters to the idle rich?' she sputtered as he hurried her on to the promenade. 'What's so funny, Mr Morgan? Who else could afford to come all the way out to a beach for lunch in November...' Her angry words drifted into silence as Cade dragged her inside a large, rather barren room.

'What is this place?' she demanded. 'It looks like a cafeteria.'

'Great deduction, Padgett. It *is* a cafeteria. And it's not polite to stare. You don't want to make all these idle rich folks uncomfortable. Do you want french fries with your chowder?'

'French...? No, no french fries.' Her voice dropped to a whisper. 'Cade, everybody here must be over seventy.'

'Yup. I first drifted into this place about three years ago when I did a concert at the outdoor theatre here on the Bay. It turns out that senior citizens flock here during the off-season.' He tilted his head towards hers and winked. 'They're a nice bunch, but not exactly fans of mine, Padgett.'

'I'm sure that's one of life's tragedies, Cade, but . . .'

He sighed and rolled his eyes heavenward. 'Jesus, woman, you can be dense! No one ever recognises me here, don't you understand? These people probably never even heard of the Marauders, so unless I showed up in black tie with an entire symphony orchestra trailing after me, nobody would even look at me twice. I can walk along the beach and stop here for chowder and . . . Look, why don't you grab that table near the window while I get our lunch?'

She watched as Cade moved from counter to counter, accumulating paper cups and dishes on his tray. Her stomach rumbled at the faint smell of coffee that hung in the air. The truth was that she was starved, but she wasn't about to let him know it. The nerve of the man, riding away with her as if he were a Hun on horseback! She'd screamed at him to turn back, but by then they were starting across the 59th Street Bridge and the sounds of the wind and the Harley and the road all conspired against her. She'd tried, of course, leaning into Cade's back until she was plastered to him, her mouth almost against his ear, her arms clutching at the hard muscles of his abdomen . . .

'You see? Just five minutes at the beach, and there's a glow in your cheeks,' he said triumphantly, setting the tray down on the table. 'Almost a blush.'

'One hour, Cade,' she said quietly. 'One hour, and then I expect you to take me back to the city.'

'Just dig in, Padgett. I got you some french fries, just in case you change your mind.'

'I won't. I never eat greasy things. And what's that?'
she asked, poking at a plastic-wrapped square of
darkish cake. 'A brownie?' Her voice rose in disbelief.
'Only a true junk-food junkie would eat something like
that. It's pure sugar.'

'I told you,' he said cheerfully, sprinkling salt on both
bags of fries, 'I'm the gourmet of roadside diners. Some
day, I'm gonna give them ratings. One star to four, only
I'll use antacid tablets instead of stars. Are you going to
eat your chowder or do I have to spoon it into you?'

'I never eat lunch. I have to watch my weight.'

'I'll watch it for you. Eat.'

'Anyway, I don't like chowder.'

'Don't like chowder?' He stared at her as if she'd
spoken heresy. 'How can anybody not like chowder?'

'It's easy,' she said, and then she sighed in defeat. 'OK,
one mouthful, just to shut you up.' Quickly, she spooned
some of the soup into her mouth and swallowed it. 'But
I'm telling you I don't...' A surprised look settled on her
face at the sudden taste of the sea and she eyed the bowl
warily. 'Well, I'll admit, that's not as bad as most. Not
that it's good, mind you.'

'Eat,' Cade ordered again.

Her stomach growled in agreement. With a resigned
sigh, she began to eat her soup. It was warm and soothing, and almost immediately she felt the tension begin to
slip away. Maybe Cade had been right, she thought
grudgingly, glancing at him from under her lashes. After all, she hadn't had a thing since coffee break, and not
then, either, she remembered suddenly. She'd been busy
with a costume fitting. And the soup really was good. It
was thick with clams and potatoes and chunks of tom-
atoes...

'Er—did you say I could have a few of those french
fries?' she asked politely.

Cade grinned. 'What I said was that one bag was
yours.'

Shannon grinned in return. 'OK, I give up. The chowder's good and I love french fries. The greasier the better.'

He leaned back in his chair and nodded his head. 'Yeah, I thought so,' he said with a smile. 'You look like a greasy french-fry type.'

'Terrific,' she muttered, eyeing him warily. 'Exactly what does that mean?'

'It means you look like the kind of woman a man can relax with. It means what you really want is to take your shoes off and walk along the sand with me. It means...'

'It means I really want that brownie, too,' she laughed. 'Especially if it's got fudge icing.'

'That is truly decadent,' Cade declared solemnly, handing the cake to her.

She was groaning by the time they'd finished eating. 'I'll never be able to fit into any of my costumes tomorrow,' she said as they padded barefoot through the sand. 'Actually, I may not have anything to worry about. I could be out of a job by then.'

Cade took her hand and laced his fingers through hers. 'Don't be silly. Jerry was just angry at how the day went. Tomorrow will be fine. You'll see.'

'I want it to be fine, Cade. That's why I've got to get home and get to work. I admit, this was fun, but...'

'Fun? Fun? Is that what you think this is, Miss Padgett?' Cade swung to face her and frowned. 'For shame, my dear,' he said dramatically. 'I thought you understood. This is a workshop exercise. Eli would approve.'

'Sure,' she said, smiling at him.

'Do I detect a note of doubt in your voice? Eli encourages his students to get inside their characters, doesn't he? Identify with them?'

'Well, yes, but...'

'So we're identifying, Padgett. I'm the old-fashioned sort, you see. I thought it would be a good idea if we got to know each other a little better before I take you to bed tomorrow. I tell you, this acting business is rough.'

Shannon laughed softly. 'I see. So this is strictly a working day, hmm?'

'No, not strictly,' he said with a quick grin. 'It's also therapeutic. And it's working—you just laughed for the first time all week.'

'Well, why wouldn't I? This is a nice place.'

'Nice? White bread is nice, Padgett. Scrambled eggs are nice. A record that can't quite make it to the top of the charts is nice . . .'

'All right, it's beautiful,' she laughed. 'Is that better?'

He grinned and squeezed her hand. 'Damned right it's beautiful. You had me worried there for a minute. Here I bring you all the way out to one of my favourite places in the world and . . . Hey, I've got a great idea! Did you ever build sand-castles when you were a kid?'

'Sand-castles? Cade, we've got to get back.'

'God, the woman is impossible! Just answer the question, Padgett. Did you ever build sand-castles?'

Shannon sighed and shook her head. 'No,' she said slowly. 'I never did.'

Dropping to his knees, he pulled her down beside him. 'I thought I had a disadvantaged childhood. Yours must have been worse.'

'I grew up in Kansas,' she said patiently, sitting back on her heels and watching him. 'It's a bit far from the beach.'

'That's right, I remember. With all those blushing female relatives. Well, where I come from, you learned to build sand-castles.'

'It figures. What else would you do in California?'

He threw back his head and laughed. 'California? I grew up in Newark, New Jersey. Right in the shadow of the Jersey Turnpike.'

'But I read somewhere . . . Not true, huh?'

Cade shook his head. 'Not even close. But one summer my mother got me into a programme for city kids and I spent a week at the New Jersey shore. The family that I stayed with had a house right on the beach. God, it was a terrific seven days! I learned to roast hot dogs over an open fire and swim...'

'And make sand-castles?'

He grinned. 'Not just sand-castles. Sand extravaganzas. Want to learn?'

'Cade, I've really got to go back to the city.'

'Sure,' he said pleasantly. 'Go on. I showed you which way to go.'

He ducked as she flung a handful of sand at him. 'I'll ignore that act of violence for the time being, Padgett. Pay attention, now. All you need is something to carry water—this cup will be fine—and a little imagination. And then, you pick the perfect spot—right about here should do it. We'll have to make strong fortifications, though. I get the feeling that a really big wave washes up here once in a while.'

Shannon watched in silence while he began scooping up handfuls of the fine white sand and flinging it aside. Finally, she shook her head.

'Are you crazy?'

'OK, don't help me. See if I care! I built my best castles without girls, anyway. Girls don't know the first thing about defences and walls and turrets. Girls...' He ducked as a mussel shell hit him on the shoulder. 'Second act of violence. Three strikes and you're out.'

'Girls—even in Kansas—build mud pies and play with clay. And we know all about turrets. After all, did you ever hear of princes getting locked away in castles? It's always princesses, isn't it? Rapunzel and Sleeping Beauty and...go on, Morgan, shove over,' she said, pushing up her sleeves and kneeling opposite him. 'I'll build you a castle the likes of which you've never seen before. Just don't get in my way.'

Ignoring Cade's snort of disbelief, Shannon began to dig in earnest. The top layer of sand was sun-warm under her fingers, but as she dug deeper, it became pleasantly cool and damp to the touch. She glanced at him as she worked; he was concentrating on his piece of the sand sculpture with the same intensity he seemed to bring to everything. It was what she'd seen in his performance that night at the Coliseum, and it was what had impressed her most during the time they'd spent together on the set and at the workshop. Was it that intensity that he brought to their love scene, she wondered suddenly, or was it something else?

'How's it coming, Padgett? Ready to admit that all the engineers in the world should be men?'

She gave him her number one nasty smile. 'Go on, laugh. Just wait until the first wave comes in. We'll see who's the better builder.'

Maybe his walls were stronger-looking, she thought, glancing from her piece of the castle to his, but her turrets were more imaginative. Surely that was important. Turrets were...

'Rats!' she shrieked, scrambling to her feet as a sudden wave engulfed the shoreline, racing across her bare feet and ankles. The water was so cold that it took her breath away, but all that mattered was that it knocked down a piece of her wall. She fell back to the wet sand and touched the damaged structure with one finger. 'Cade,' she wailed, 'look what happened!'

He sighed dramatically as he knelt beside her. 'I should have known a woman couldn't compete in a man's game. You faked me out with that bit about mud pies, but what's a mud pie, after all? It doesn't require a man's skill and talent. It... Hey, no fair, Padgett, cut it out!' Her first handful of sand missed its target, but the second sprayed over his shoulders and face. 'Can't take the truth, huh?' he laughed, reaching for her hands. 'Is that your problem?'

'You're a male chauvinist pig, Cade Morgan. That wave came in and headed straight for me... Cade, don't! Come on, that's not fair! Cade...' With a shriek of laughter, Shannon tried to roll free of his grasp, but he pulled her down to the sand and stuffed a handful of the damp stuff down her collar. 'That's not fair... Cade...'

'Damned right it's not,' he laughed, throwing his leg across her and pinning her body beneath his. 'Men build better castles than women, Padgett. They're also bigger and stronger.'

'That's it,' she gasped, 'if you can't win fair and square, win by intimidation.'

She was laughing up at him, squirming beneath his weight like a kid in a wrestling match when suddenly the laughter caught in her throat. Cade's eyes met hers; the gleam in them faded, replaced by a dark intensity that made something stir deep within her.

'Cade... let me up.'

Her plea was a whisper, a husky sigh on the salty breeze. He shook his head.

'You're beautiful, Shannon,' he said softly. 'My fairy-tale princess with sand on her cheeks.'

She drew in her breath as he reached out and stroked her face. Her skin felt as if it were glowing beneath his fingers. What would he do if she turned her head and pressed her mouth to his palm, she wondered suddenly? Would he take her into his arms and kiss her? Would he make love to her here on the empty beach, with only the gulls to see them while the ocean roared and the wind cooled their passion-heated flesh?

'Let me get up,' she pleaded.

'Listen,' he said, and she could hear a touch of urgency in his voice, 'listen, forget the damned play.'

'What?' She closed her eyes and then opened them again. 'I'm not thinking of the play. I...'

'I don't mean right now, Shannon. I mean... Just stop thinking of us as characters on a set.' His body stirred against hers, and he bent towards her until she could feel the warmth of his breath against her face. 'Isn't it time we faced the truth? I want to make love to you—and you want that, too. You know you do. That's why you can't play that damned scene.'

'Don't be ridiculous. The scene embarrasses me, that's all. It was the same with Tony.'

'The hell it was the same with Tony! You're scared to play the scene with me because you're scared of feeling something.'

She turned her face away from his. 'Acting doesn't involve feeling, Cade. Acting is . . .'

'What we feel for each other hasn't got a damned thing to do with acting,' he growled, cupping her chin in his hand and forcing her face towards his. 'And we both know it.

She took a shuddering breath. 'Don't you see how artificial all this is? Jerry Crawford brought us together.'

'Don't tell me we're back to that?'

Shannon shook her head. 'That's not what I meant. You know I've already admitted you're a pretty good actor.'

'Pretty good?'

'Look, you're not what I expected, OK? But you've got to admit you wouldn't have this part if it weren't for Jerry throwing us together.'

'Crawford's not responsible for what we feel, Shannon.'

She took a deep breath. 'Cade, I've seen this kind of thing before. People meet during a play or a film, they have some kind of stage relationship and . . .'

'Damn it, is that all you think this is?'

'You're new to the theatre,' she said, deliberately not giving him an answer. 'You don't know how easy it is to get trapped inside a part. It's a common problem. Al Pacino spoke at the workshop once—he talked about how he felt while he was filming *The Godfather*. He said he was like a different person for a while and . . .'

'Don't tell me you think what we feel is mixed up with the parts we're playing.'

'I'm telling you that I've seen this kind of thing before. It's easy to confuse fantasy and reality.'

Cade's eyes searched hers. 'Some guy did a number on you, didn't he?' he asked softly.

'If you mean have I been through this myself,' she said, taking a deep breath, 'the answer is yes. When I was in my first summer stock company. I played Juliet and I . . . I . . .'

'I knew it,' he said. 'Listen, I'm not that two-cent Romeo. That bastard . . .'

'He wasn't a bastard,' she said softly. 'He was just a lesson well learned.' She swallowed and forced a smile to her face. 'You and I are lucky, Cade. We're able to bring something special to our scenes together.'

'And that's all it is?' He clasped her shoulders and stared at her, his eyes that indigo mystery that she feared. A thin smile crossed his face. 'And that's all you want, Shannon?'

No, she thought suddenly, and her heart thudded against her ribs. But she nodded.

'Isn't that enough? We're going to be the best on-screen lovers in years. We're gonna knock 'em dead, remember?'

'I remember everything,' he said softly, reaching out and tucking a stray curl behind her ear. 'Everything.'

And so do I, she thought, recalling the feel of his mouth against hers. It was bad enough she'd have to play on-camera love scenes with him for the next four months. She certainly wasn't going to play them offstage, as well, and then have him walk away with her heart. Not even Cade Morgan was entitled to that.

'Just be sure you remember your lines tomorrow,' she said in a bright voice, scrambling away from him and getting to her feet. 'I'd hate to have to improvise dialogue and worry about that collapsing bed at the same time.'

There was enough to worry about already, she thought, turning away from him and starting back up the windswept beach. Finding a way to hide within Alana Dunbar was going to be a task that would require a talent she was uncertain she possessed.

CHAPTER EIGHT

SHANNON turned slowly in Cade's arms, nestling her head on the hard plane of his naked shoulder. Somewhere in the distance, music was playing, soft violins swelling as Cade's mouth ravaged hers.

'That's wonderful, darling,' she whispered softly, smiling up at him through half-lidded eyes. 'Wonderful.'

'Wonderful!' Jerry echoed from the sidelines. 'OK, kids, you were great. Wrap it for the day.'

Thank God, Shannon thought desperately. She pushed Cade away from her and sat up quickly. 'Excuse me,' she said, swinging her legs to the floor.

He smiled at her. 'Sure,' he said softly.

Her eyes met his briefly and then she looked past him, towards the perimeter of the set. She could see her robe lying across an unused camera. But to get to it, she'd have to let go of the sheet she was clutching and then walk across the set in her bodysuit while Cade sat and watched.

He rose and stretched lazily. Shannon looked away from him. Think about something else, she told herself. Think about all you have to do when you get home tonight. The laundry and the cleaning and...

'Here,' he said politely.

She looked up in surprise. Cade was holding her robe out to her. 'I...thank you,' she said with equal politeness, taking it from him and scrambling into it.

'You're welcome,' he said solemnly.

But there was nothing solemn about the way he was looking at her. There was a gleam in his eyes, a twitch at the corner of his mouth...

'You guys were terrific,' Jerry said, beaming at them. He slapped Shannon on the back and grinned. 'What a performance!'

Shannon rose from the bed, avoiding Cade's eyes as each of them murmured their thanks. Crawford had been complimenting them all week, telling them and the network publicity department that he'd never seen such chemistry before. He'd been delighted ever since the day they'd finally played that first love scene together.

'Spontaneous combustion,' he'd said, and Shannon had avoided Cade's eyes then, too, because she knew he'd figured out the truth, even if Jerry hadn't. It hadn't been spontaneous combustion. The sparks Jerry had wanted were there, but they were phonies. Shannon had given the best performance of her life and she'd gone on doing it every day since. She'd only lost her concentration once, only let herself feel Cade's arms and Cade's body and Cade's mouth one time and that had happened today, damn it, today, and she didn't know how she'd let herself slip that way...

'Shannon? I want you in early Monday. The network wants to get some publicity stills of you two.'

She cleared her throat and nodded. 'Yes, OK, Jerry. I'll be here. Er—if we're done for the day...?'

'Sure, sure, you can go. Cade, can I have a minute?'

'I'm in a bit of a hurry, Jerry.'

'I'll make it fast,' the director promised.

Not too fast, Shannon thought, risking a quick glance at Cade as he reached for his shirt. Give me time enough to get away. His head swung towards her, his eyes catching hers for an instant. His slow smile brought a momentary rush of confusion and she swivelled sharply on her heel and hurried towards her dressing-room, determined to be in her street clothes and out of the studio before he could stop her.

Her shoulders sagged with relief as she slammed the dressing-room door behind her. Well, she thought, another day and she'd survived. She sighed as she peeled off her bodysuit. At least there were no gawkers standing around the set any more when she and Cade played their love scenes. Cade had seen to that the day after their afternoon at the beach.

'I want the set cleared,' he'd said to Jerry. 'We don't need anybody watching but the technicians.' His voice had been soft, but there was no doubt in Shannon's mind that it was a command, not a request. 'That should make things easier,' he'd said to her with a quick smile, and she'd nodded, for once in her life grateful that stars had certain prerogatives denied to mere mortals.

And it *had* made things easier. The cleared set, the tiny but private dressing-room—all of it helped her get through the day. And when Cade became persistent, when he tried to talk to her about what was happening each time he took her in his arms, she pretended ignorance.

'You're one hell of an actress, Padgett,' he'd said the day before. 'You've even got Jerry convinced—he asked me if we're seeing each other.'

'You told him the truth, I hope,' she'd said quickly.

Cade had grinned lazily. 'I said I wished we were. Nothing more.'

'There isn't any more.'

'Sure there is. I could have told him you're the amazing mechanical woman. You walk and talk and you even breathe heavily on cue. You've made everybody a believer. Even Jerry. But then, Jerry's not in bed with you.'

'Damn it, Cade . . .'

'That's a hell of a trick, you know. I reach for you and I end up with Alana Dunbar.'

Shannon had taken a deep breath. 'I tried to tell you, Cade—the woman in that bed *is* Alana Dunbar.'

His fingers had curled around her wrist. 'Prove it. Spend an evening with me. Let me take you to dinner.'

'No.'

'To a movie, then.'

'I'm busy.'

'Then we'll make it tomorrow night . . .'

'I'm busy then, too.'

'Sure you are.'

'I am,' she'd insisted. 'I . . .'

'You're afraid,' he'd said softly.

'That's crazy,' she'd answered. 'I'm just doing my job.'

And one damned fine job it had been until the last take, she thought grimly, stripping off the hated body-suit and tossing it in the corner. Well, at least it was Friday. That meant two days away from this pressure cooker. She sighed as she slipped into a pair of old corduroys and an oversized sweater. She'd sleep late and soak in the tub and maybe even indulge herself in cooking up a real meal—*linguine* with lobster sauce or chicken kiev, and to hell with the calories and what an extra pound or two would look like through the camera's critical eye—and then on Monday, she'd be in control again.

Wearily, she slumped into the chair before her dressing-table and stared at her reflection in the mirror. Alana Dunbar stared back at her, with her crimson lips and gilded eyelids. So long, Alana, Shannon thought, reaching for the cold cream. You can rest over the weekend, but I expect you to be ready for work first thing Monday morning. You can do it, Alana. You know you can. You've done fine all week, ever since that day at the beach.

That day had sent her home in a state of panic. She'd masked it from Cade, turning down his suggestion of dinner, maintaining her poise until she was up the stairs and safely in her apartment. Then she'd let go, flying to the telephone and dialling Claire's number before she was out of her jacket.

'What would happen if I quit the soap?' she had asked without preamble.

'Nothing much,' Claire had said carefully. 'We'd get sued for breach of contract, but don't worry about it. I've always had this burning desire to manage a troupe of trained fleas, and I'm sure you can land a great job demonstrating pots and pans at Macy's. What's the problem, sweetie?'

'Problem? Did I say there was a problem?' Shannon had snarled, slamming down the phone. 'Why should there be a problem?' she'd demanded of the high-ceilinged rooms. Anyway, quitting *All Our Tomorrows* was out of the question. You didn't toss aside a career because you couldn't handle one stupid love scene.

She had paused in her pacing long enough to pour herself a glass of cream sherry. Love scene, singular? she'd thought, tossing the sherry back and coughing as it hit her throat. Try multiplying that by a zillion. Not that she'd seen the story-board—it was guarded like a state secret—but only a simpleton would believe that the writers were going to suddenly turn Alana Dunbar and Johnny Wolff into celibates. Which was, of course, all the more reason why she had to figure out how to get through the damned scene, because if she could make it through one, she could make it through as many as they tossed at her.

She'd swallowed the sherry and poured herself more, wondering briefly what her mother would say if she could see her daughter belting the stuff down as if it were iced tea on a summer day. What would she think when she tuned in *All Our Tomorrows* and saw her daughter melting in the arms of Cade Morgan? That was a better question!

If only she'd carried off that dumb love scene with Tony. Those damned laundry lists dancing through her head had done her in. Why had she let her mind drift to such mundane things? That had never happened to her before... Well, yes, once a long time ago, but then it had been deliberate. She'd had a part in an off-Broadway play and had to strip down to her teddy.

'I'll die of embarrassment,' she'd moaned to Eli, and he'd taught her an exercise that required thinking about something dull to help maintain concentration while separating yourself from the actions of your character. And it had worked; thinking about laundry had got her through.

The sherry had sloshed over the edge of the glass and a trickle of amber drops had traced a path across her hand. Was it really that simple? Had the solution been there all along? Shannon had taken a deep breath and set the glass down on the kitchen counter. God, how had she missed it? If she kept half her mind occupied with trivia and the other half busy with camera angles and cues and lines, there'd be no part of her left to think about...about whatever Cade was doing. Reach into yourself, Eli always said, and use what you find.

She'd traded the sherry bottle for a pot of double-strength coffee, and then she'd sat up half the night, gulping the bitter black liquid and reviewing everything she knew about acting technique and control. And it had worked. Nobody suspected a thing. Nobody but Cade...

'Shannon? Are you there?'

She blinked as the light tap on the door was repeated. *That's what I get for day-dreaming. I should have been long gone by now.*

'I was just leaving,' she said, grabbing her jacket. 'I have...'

The door swung open and she stared into the mirror. Cade stood behind her, a scowl on his handsome face.

'You have an appointment, I know.' A quick response sprang to her lips but she hesitated, caught by the troubled look on his face. 'Shannon, have you seen the script changes for Monday?'

She shook her head as he handed her a thin sheaf of papers. 'I haven't, no. I know Jerry said there would be some. Is something wrong?'

Cade ran his fingers through his hair. 'Not unless you find fault with a graveside seduction,' he sighed. 'Jerry thinks it's great.'

'Graveside sed...? What are you talking about?' she demanded, leafing through the pages he'd given her. 'I thought we were going to do the Dunbar funeral, the cemetery scene—complete with fog machines—and then the reading of Alana's father's will.'

Cade nodded his head. 'Oh, we are. But take a look at page four, Padgett. How am I supposed to deliver those lines? "I'll take you home and kiss the sadness from your beautiful eyes..." Jesus, who's kidding who? I know Johnny Wolff is supposed to be the sexiest SOB in the world, but even Alana Dunbar would spit in his eye if he came on to her at her father's funeral.'

'Ours not to reason why, Cade, ours just to do...'

'Or die. Yeah, and that's what I'm afraid of—dying out there on coast-to-coast TV. This is supposed to be the start of the new Cade Morgan, not the finish. What comic wrote those lines, anyway?'

Shannon shuffled through the script. 'My God,' she muttered, 'have you seen Alana's answer? You're getting off easy. I have to smile from behind my black veil and whisper—where is it again?—I have to say, "Yes, Johnny, yes, make me fly away, make me forget this awful place." Can you just hear Alana saying that with daddy lying in the grave at her feet?'

Cade groaned softly. 'Are you sure this isn't somebody's idea of a joke? Damn it, Padgett, by the time we get to the reading of the will, I'll be so sick that I'll wish I were in old man Dunbar's casket.'

'You can't do that, Cade. You've got to become Johnny—you've got to believe in him just as he's written.'

'I just don't think I can handle it.' He caught his lip between his teeth and drew in his breath. 'Look, I don't want to drag you down with me. I—er—I thought I'd drop by the workshop and talk to Eli...'

'You can't do that. He's still on the road with the Shepherd play.'

'Damn, I forgot. Well, don't worry about it, Padgett.' He hesitated, then shrugged his shoulders. 'What the hell, I'll do the best I can. It's my problem, not yours.'

She handed him the script and smiled encouragingly. 'I admit it's a bad scene, but we'll manage. Stop worrying.'

'I wish I had your confidence.' Cade's shoulders slumped. 'I—er—I suppose you've got a million appointments to keep, hmm? I mean, I guess you don't have time to sit here and cheer me up.'

Lord, she thought, glancing up at his woebegone expression, he looks almost as terrified as he did that first day in the workshop.

'That's all right,' she said gently. 'I'm not in any particular rush.'

''You mean, you haven't got any appointments today?'

'No,' she said without thinking, 'none at...' The words caught in her throat as a triumphant grin flashed across his face. 'Now, Cade...'

'Gotcha fair and square, Padgett. You've had something or other to keep you busy every day for the past week.'

'I have a crowded schedule. I...'

'Yeah, I know. If there were twenty-five hours in a day, you'd be busy twenty-six of them. Day and night classes, night and day appointments...'

'I can't help that. I...'

'Busy, busy, busy. Except for today.'

She shook her head. 'I simply meant I could spare a few minutes to talk. Of course I'm busy today—I've got to work on my part.'

'Amazing,' he said softly. 'So do I.'

'There's no benefit to our working together,' she said quickly.

Cade nodded in agreement. 'Oh, absolutely right,' he agreed solemnly. 'What possible use could there be if two people who are going to play a scene together studied it together?'

'All each of us has to do is memorise some lines,' she said helplessly as the trap shut around her. 'There's nothing much to that.'

'Right. We wouldn't want to risk finding some way to make the damned lines make some kind of sense. It's much better to handle this separately. So, what's Monday's game plan, Padgett? Shall we both blow our lines, or are you going to come up with something brilliant while I come on the set and do a stand-up comedy routine?' He waggled his eyebrows and raised an imaginary cigar to his mouth. 'A funny thing happened to me on the way to the cemetery,' he said out of the side of his mouth.

'Cade, come on, you'll do fine.'

'A young lady asked me to make love to her on a coffin and I told her she didn't have a ghost of a chance.'

She laughed softly. 'Stop that. Look, all you have to do is say the lines straight.'

'"I love you when you wear sexy black stock certificates, Alana..."'

'Come on, Cade. That's not in the script and you know it.'

'I don't want you to feel guilty when I get laughed off the set, Padgett. It won't be your fault. Just because you turned me down when I pleaded for help...'

'Cade...'

'I can picture the *Enquirer* headline now,' he said dreamily. '"Morgan Murders Moving Moment". Well, that would be better than "Padgett and Morgan Kill Careers on National TV". Of course, I'd see to it they spelled your name right.'

'OK, OK, you win,' she said quickly, glancing at her watch. 'One hour, all right? Go dredge up another copy of the script.'

'I've got one in my dressing-room.'

'Well then, go get it and we'll read lines together.'

'We can't read here,' he said patiently. She looked up at him sharply and he shrugged his shoulders, eyes wide with innocence. 'Look, it's not my fault. They're going to be constructing a new set today.' As if on cue, the high-pitched whine of an electric drill pierced the air. 'So, unless you want to compete with that . . .'

'Why do I feel as if I've been set up?' Shannon sighed.

The sounds of the drill were augmented by the thud of a hammer.

'Look, I know what you're thinking, Padgett. Well, you're in for a surprise. I am not going to suggest we rehearse at my place.'

'Gosh,' she said with studied innocence, "I never even thought of that.'

'Nor am I going to suggest your place.'

'Good, because my apartment's out of the question. And I am absolutely, positively not going to the beach. All of which leaves us nowhere.'

'Ah, what little faith you have in me, woman. I know the perfect spot. It's close by, it's entirely public, but no one will think we're nuts when we start reading lines from Monday's black comedy.'

Shannon made a face. 'Sure,' she said. 'And I'm Mickey Mouse.'

Cade grinned and tapped her nose lightly with his finger. 'Only when you've got your slippers on,' he said. 'Anyway, I think of you as Minnie. Even dear, dead, daddy Dunbar would see the difference.'

* * *

'The Staten Island Ferry?' Shannon grumbled as she watched Cade chain up his motorcycle. 'What kind of place is that for reading lines?'

'I told you, it's the perfect place. Trust me.'

'Hah! I remember all too well the last time I did that, Mr Morgan. I ended up a kidnap victim...'

'Now, now, Padgett,' he said, taking her hand in his and tugging her along after him towards the railing. 'I simply took you to the beach and then brought you back to the city, safe and sound and...'

'Cade...'

'...and ready to take on the next day's taping. Which is what's going to happen after our ferry ride across the Bay.'

'Damn it, Cade, nobody goes to Staten Island.'

'Try telling that to the New Yorkers who live there.'

'And nobody rides the ferry in this kind of weather. It's cold.'

'You're wearing a down jacket, aren't you?'

Shannon clucked her tongue in exasperation. 'And it's foggy.'

'Just the way it's going to be on the set when Murray gets that fog machine going. I thought you were a believer in method acting.

'When you put it that way,' she said sarcastically, 'I can't imagine why I didn't think of it myself.'

'Listen, this is the greatest sea voyage in the world, Padgett,' Cade said, slipping a protective arm lightly around her shoulders as the *American Legion* lurched out of its slip and crept cautiously into the fog enveloping Manhattan Bay. 'I spent a lot of time on these boats when I was first starting out.'

She shivered in a gust of salt-laden air and Cade glanced down at her. 'Is it too cool for you? We can ride inside, if you like.'

Shannon shook her head and brushed a strand of hair out of her eyes. 'If we're going to take an ocean voyage,

I want to take advantage of it.' She looked at him and gave him a quick smile. 'Don't let it go to your head, but this isn't bad. I can smell the sea—and I don't think I've been anywhere in New York that's this empty.' Pulling up her jacket collar, she moved out of his encircling arm and turned her back to the wind. 'OK, Morgan, let's read. We'll make sense out of this scene yet.'

'Well,' Cade sighed twenty mnutes later, 'at least it sounds a little better. I didn't think there were so many different ways to read a line.

'It's my chattering teeth that make them sound different,' Shannon laughed. 'God, it's cold!'

'That's it,' Cade said, slipping his arm around her. 'We're going inside.'

'No, don't be silly. Really, I like it out here.' She tucked a blowing strand of hair behind her ear and looked up at him. 'What did you mean when you said you used to spend a lot of time on the ferry? Did you live on Staten Island?'

He laughed softly. 'Nobody lives on Staten Island, remember? Sure, I took a hole-in-the-wall apartment down near the docks after I left Princeton. One room, make your own heat and hot water, cockroaches are free— sometimes, when I'd feel about as far down as I could get, I'd grab my guitar and ride the ferry.'

'Left Princeton? Not "graduated"?'

Cade shrugged his shoulders. 'I gave it up when I had less than a year to go. I was eager to get out into the real world, I guess...Well, it was more than that. My mother had just died and I felt, I don't know, I felt as if nothing really mattered much.

'What about your father?'

'What about him?' He gave her a quick smile. 'I don't mean to sound bitter, but I never knew my father. He took off when I was little. My mother worked all her life to keep a roof over our heads. God, I can still remember the Christmas she gave me my first guitar.' Cade's eyes darkened with painful memory. 'It probably cost her six months of overtime.'

Shannon fought against the desire to reach up and smooth the lines of tension from his face. 'And the rest, as they say, is history?' she said lightly.

He laughed and squeezed her shoulder gratefully. 'Something like that. Anyway, when I lived in Staten Island, the ferry became my emotional escape route. I used to ride it for hours.'

'All by yourself?'

He nodded. 'Yeah, just me and my guitar. The smell of the sea and the sound of the gulls were—I don't know, they were enough to make me feel human again. After a while, some of the guys who worked the ferries got to know me, and they'd let me ride back and forth for one nickel. That's all it cost then, just five cents for an ocean cruise that was better than any hour spent with a shrink.' He glanced down at her and laughed self-consciously. 'It really is a great place to rehearse, you know. I wrote my first hit on the ferry... Damn, Padgett, why don't you tell me to shut up? I sound like a nostalgia trip.'

'*Sea Lover?* Written on this boat? Do you know, I can still remember the first time I heard it. I was taking a summer school course in English Lit, and our assignment was to pick a contemporary poem and present it to the class.' She dipped her head and looked away in sudden embarrassment. 'I chose *Sea Lover.* Just the words, you know, as if it were a poem and not a song. I thought it was beautiful.'

'My first hit,' he said, smiling at her. 'Did you really like it?'

She nodded, warmed by the sound of pleasure she heard in his voice. 'I still do. Did you really write it on the ferry? I've always pictured composers working in sound-proofed studios.'

'Maybe some do. I just need a quiet place I can call my own, somewhere I can smell the ocean and hear the sound of the sea.' He smiled down at her and tucked a strand of dark hair behind her ear. 'I guess we don't know much about the other's profession, do we? I mean, I'd never have thought actors in soaps put in so many hours each day.'

'Not all of them do,' Shannon said. 'Rima just floats in and out.'

'Rima's not an actress, she's a happening.' They both laughed and then Cade sighed. 'You're the actress, Padgett. You're good enough to carry both of us.'

'You don't need me to carry you, Cade.'

'Look, let's be honest. I'd have made an ass of myself a dozen times over if you weren't there.'

'That's not true,' she said quickly. 'You're good. Even Eli says so.'

He smiled and shrugged his shoulders. 'Yeah, but where is Eli when I need him?'

'Don't worry about Monday. You'll be fine.'

'I'll be a human laughing machine.'

'No, you won't be,' Shannon said with determination. 'I'll teach you some tricks of the trade. For instance, think of something sad when you're playing a sad scene. It really helps a lot.'

'The only sad thing I can think of when I look at Monday's dialogue is that it's going to be the end of my short but awful career.'

'No—try to think of something positive.'

'Unemployment insurance,' he said promptly, and Shannon chuckled.

'You're impossible,' she said. 'And crazy.'

'Right and right, but mostly, I'm scared stiff. You don't know how much this job means to me. I'm getting kind of old for one-night stands...' He glanced down at her and laughed softly at the look on her face. 'Concert performances, Padgett. I gave up the other kind a long time ago.'

'Really?' she asked, her voice a study in disinterest.

He nodded. 'Really. There's something terribly sad in waking up and finding you can't recall the name of the girl lying beside you. Maybe it was exciting when I was twenty, but at thirty it was depressing as hell. What's even worse is having to phone the desk clerk to ask what town you're in.'

'I take it life on the road isn't as glamorous as the Sunday supplements make it sound.'

Cade's laughter was harsh. 'It's not what it's cracked up to be, no.'

Shannon moved away from him and leaned her elbows on the deck railing. 'Neither is acting. When I was growing up, I used to read articles about people like Jane Fonda and picture myself signing autographs and giving interviews. Nobody told me about the cattle calls—you know, the open auditions where a couple of hundred actresses show up for one part. They never told me about how often you come close to starving.'

'I know I'm lucky to have avoided all that,' he said quickly, almost defensively. 'You worked hard to get where you are and I just kind of wandered in.'

It was what she had told herself from the first, but now it no longer seemed quite that simple. There was an embarrassed smile on her face as she turned towards him.

'I suppose we just came at it from different directions,' she said slowly. 'You worked hard to get where you are.'

'You don't have to be charitable, Shannon.'

'No, no, I mean it. You're a fine musician.'

'Not just a guitar player?' he asked gently.

A rush of crimson rose to her cheeks. 'I shouldn't have said that. But I was angry that day. It wasn't just you, Cade. Part of it was Rima, and the way everybody walks on eggs around her because she has a name. And then you came along and suddenly Jerry was all smiles... I admit, I wasn't terribly happy to see you.'

'No kidding,' he said, smiling at her.

'But it had nothing to do with your music,' she said quickly. 'The truth is, I've always liked your songs. They say things I feel . . .'

She broke off and turned away from him, looking down at the foam flecked water slipping by the hull. She'd said more than she'd intended. She sensed him moving closer to her and her heart began to race. He put a hand on the railing on either side of her, trapping her between his arms.

'What things?' he asked softly.

Tell him, she thought, tell him everything. Tell him you hear his loneliness and understand it. Tell him he's like his music, strong yet tender at the same time. Tell him how hard it is not to surrender each time he kisses you...

'Shannon?' he whispered. She could feel his breath against the nape of her neck, the warmth of it heating her wind-chilled flesh. 'I wanted to tell you . . . This week, being with you every day, working with you . . . I couldn't have done it without you.'

Of course, she thought, closing her eyes as his voice murmured softly to her. She was his ticket to success, the end to those nights and days and weeks on the road. Everything else was make-believe.

With a groan, the ferry bumped into its Staten Island slip. Shannon staggered backward, falling against Cade momentarily as the deck lurched beneath their feet.

'Careful,' he said, holding her lightly against him. 'You don't want to fall.'

How right he was, she thought, staring blindly into the fog. With Cade Morgan, it would be all too easy.

CHAPTER NINE

THE Greek restaurant on 15th Street was, as Cade had promised, a warm oasis in the damp November evening.

'We both have to eat, don't we?' he'd said. 'It might as well be together—unless you can't bear the thought of real food instead of a TV dinner.'

'I suppose I can survive one night without dining on plastic chicken,' Shannon had laughed. After all, she'd thought as she clung to him on the back of the Harley, what harm could come of having dinner together?

A string of tin bells strung over the door tinkled as they entered the restaurant, the bright tones barely audible over the soft buzz of conversation coming from the small bar to the right. A few gnarled faces looked up as the door closed behind them, glancing at Shannon and Cade with indifference. Beyond, dark wooden booths clung to rough, whitewashed walls. The air was delicately scented with garlic and rosemary.

'Are you sure we're in Manhattan?' Shannon whispered as Cade slipped her jacket from her shoulders.

'Every sea voyage should end at a foreign port,' he said softly. 'Just wait until you taste Elena's grilled lamb. *Yasou,* Nico,' he called, stepping towards a straight-backed old man with a fierce smile and a headful of white curls. 'It's good to see you again.'

The old man smiled. '*Yasou,* my friend. It is a long time.'

Cade smiled as he slipped his arm around Shannon. 'This is Miss Padgett. I've been telling her all about the magic of Elena's kitchen.'

Shannon smiled as the old man took her hand in his. 'Cade's managed to make everything sound wonderful, although I'm afraid I don't know much about Greek food.'

'Then it will be our pleasure to teach you, Miss Padgett.'

'Where is Elena?' Cade asked.

'Where am I always?' a musical voice chuckled. '*Kahleespehrah*, Cade. We have missed you.'

Cade grinned as he kissed the cheek she offered him. 'Good evening to you as well, Elena. You're beautiful, as always.'

The woman laughed and patted his cheek. 'You are a good liar, as always.' Her dark eyes slid to Shannon and she smiled. 'Nico, why do you let our guests stand here like this? Take Cade to his table and bring them some retsina while I go to the kitchen. What would you like, Cade? I have some wonderful little fish I can grill, and those meatballs you love, with the lemon sauce. And I made *musakas* just this afternoon.'

'Whatever you choose, Elena. I put myself in your hands.'

'I can see why you like it here,' Shannon murmured as they settled into the farthest booth. 'They act as if the prodigal son's returned!'

'Nico and Elena are as close to family as I've got. They bought this place about the same time I put the Marauders together. Elena's half-convinced I'm their good-luck charm, although I keep telling her it's the other way around. Thank you, Nico,' he said as the old man brought them a bottle of retsina. 'This is just what we need on such a cold, wet night.'

'I think I'll pass,' Shannon said, watching as Cade poured the yellowish liquid.

'It tastes better than it looks,' he said. 'Try some of mine.'

She leaned forward obediently, sniffing at the glass he held out to her, and then she took a sip.

'Paint thinner,' she said, wrinkling her nose. 'With a touch of liquorice added so you can get it down.'

Cade laughed. 'It's easy to tell you've led a sheltered life, Padgett. I'll order some white wine.'

'No, don't, please. I'd only fall on my face. I have to confess—I'm starving, and anything I drink will go right to my head.'

'That's a tempting prospect. A foggy night and a beautiful woman, her head reeling from a bit too much to drink...'

Shannon laughed softly. 'I hate to ruin that little scene, Cade, but when this woman has too much to drink, she tends to fall on her face. At least, that's what they tell me.'

'You mean you don't remember? It's bad enough to be drunk, but to be drunk and not remember is positively sinful.'

'I remember just enough to think it's a miracle I lived,' she said, smiling at him. 'I was in my third year at college...'

'Where?'

Her smile broadened. 'Kansas State,' she said. 'Where else?'

'Where else, indeed?' he grinned. 'So, tell me the rest. You were in your junior year...'

'...and I hadn't eaten anything for three days...'

'Three days without eating? What were you doing—trying out for a part in The Invisible Man?'

'I was cramming for final exams,' she said with dignity. 'Do you really think I'd starve myself just for a part?' Cade's eyebrows arched and she laughed softly. 'OK, so I would.' She paused as Nico placed a platter on the table. 'Umm, that smells wonderful. What is it?'

'A little of this, a little of that,' the old man said with a shrug. 'Eat—but save room for the rest.'

'You mean, there's going to be more?' Shannon asked Cade in disbelief.

'I should have warned you. Elena never forgot the early days when I'd pack in a meal here in hopes it would hold me for a while. Try those little round things—the cheese pastries. And have some of the stuffed grape leaves, too.' He watched while she took her first bite. 'Good?'

'Delicious.'

'I'm glad. Now, tell me more about Kansas. Do you miss it?'

Shannon swallowed a mouthful and smiled wistfully. 'Sometimes. But I get home for holidays—well, usually. I couldn't make it last year—I was in an off-Broadway play—so my Dad packed up what looked like half the dinner my mother had made and shipped it to me Air Express. The kids in the cast and I feasted for days!'

'Your folks sound like nice people.'

She nodded. 'They are.' She looked down at the table and then back at him. 'Do you want to know something funny?' she asked softly. Cade nodded. 'I was a little concerned about . . . well, about this new part. I didn't know how they'd feel, seeing me . . . seeing you . . .' She took a breath and laughed softly. 'My mother called to tell me they were proud of me. She said I was giving a great performance.'

'Your mother and I agree completely.'

'She said it was an improvement over seeing me play a happy toadstool in first grade.' Shannon laughed and shook her head. 'So much for the sheltered folks back in Kansas, hmm?'

Cade grinned. 'Would you believe that the Marauders have never given a concert in Kansas? We gave a concert in Kansas City when we first started ten years ago, but for some stupid reason, that's in Missouri.'

'Ten years. That's a long time for a band to be together, isn't it?'

'An eternity. But we've been lucky. We get along well together.'

'What are the other Marauders doing while you're on *Tomorrows?* I can't imagine the music business is any different from acting—you've got to keep busy or they forget your face.'

'That's the truth. But we'd been talking about dissolving the band...'

Shannon stared at him. 'Dissolving it?'

'You sound like our manager,' Cade laughed. 'Maybe "dissolving" is a bit strong. It isn't as if we'd vanish. But we're all ready to try our hands at other things. Jack and Phil have been talking about opening a club and Tommy's into his latest far-Eastern guru.'

'And you decided to take a shot at acting?'

Cade pushed his plate aside. 'It wasn't quite that simple, Padgett. But Jerry gave me a chance and I figured if I were ever going to try, now was the time,, while they still know my name out there.' He smiled disarmingly. 'It's called capitalising your assets.'

She smiled in return. 'Take the money and run, huh?'

He nodded. 'Absolutely. Everything moves fast in this business. If something feels right, you've got to go for it. If I've learned nothing else in all these years, I've learned that much.'

Shannon sat back as Nico set down fresh platters of food.

'Elena says to please notice she's sent over your favourite beer, Cade, although she thinks only a barbarian would drink Mexican beer with Greek food. Still, she says you are to enjoy your meal.'

Shannon smiled as the old man shuffled off. 'Elena and Nico really are like family. Treating you as if you're still a child is a sure sign.'

Suddenly, Cade reached across the table and put his hand over hers. 'Are you glad you let me talk you into having dinner with me?'

Her eyes met his. 'Yes,' she said softly. 'I'm very glad. This has been one of the nicest days I can remember.'

'*Baklava,*' Elena interrupted proudly, 'brandy, and coffee. Have you ever had Greek coffee, Miss Padgett? No? Well, you will love it, I'm sure.'

Half an hour later, Shannon eased herself from the back of the Harley.

'I may never eat again,' she said solemnly. 'I'll bet I have trouble fitting into my sexy black Alana Dunbar funeral dress Monday.'

'I wish you hadn't reminded me,' Cade groaned. 'I'd almost forgotten that damned scene. We were going to run through it one last time.'

'We still can. Would you like to come up for a cup of coffee? Plain, black American coffee, that is. No sugar, no brandy, no calories. How does that sound?'

Surprise registered in Cade's face. 'It sounds wonderful.'

Why had she done that? Shannon wondered. The invitation had been made without thought, surprising her as much as it had surprised him. For a second, she thought of rescinding it, but Cade had already chained the motorcycle and started towards her doorway.

'Shannon?' he called, and she nodded and smiled at him.

'Coming,' she said. 'Just getting my breath for the long climb up.'

And it *was* a long climb, seemingly longer than ever before, but then, she'd never made it with Cade behind her, watching as she trotted up the stairs, brushing against her on the narrow landings, even once reaching out and grasping her waist when she stumbled on a loose step.

'I'm OK,' she said, but she wasn't. Her heart was tripping crazily, and she knew it had nothing to do with the effort of climbing the stairs.

Once in the apartment, she hurried from lamp to lamp, turning on the lights as if to exorcise the darkness. Cade sat quietly in the living-room, watching her. She glanced at him and smiled nervously.

'Coffee coming up,' she said brightly. 'I hope you like it black.'

'The way you made it the last time was fine, Shannon.'

'That was instant stuff, remember?' she called over her shoulder as she headed towards the kitchen. 'This is going to be the real thing.'

'Yes, I hope so,' he said, and she froze in her tracks.

'Cade, look,' she said tentatively, turning to face him, 'maybe this wasn't such a good idea.'

'You promised me a rehearsal and a cup of coffee,' he said easily. 'Give me both and I'll leave quietly.'

A hesitant smile tilted at the corners of her mouth. 'Promise?'

Cade grinned. 'Scout's honour,' he said solemnly. 'Trust me.'

Hours later, Shannon tossed the script aside and put her hand to her throat.

'"Yes, Johnny, yes,"' she gagged melodramatically. '"Make me fly away, make me forget this awful place…"' Arrgh,' she gasped, 'I can't do it, I can't. I'd rather kill myself than say those lines again.'

'I know what you mean,' Cade groaned. 'I think I have brain rot.'

Shannon grinned wickedly. 'Do you think Jerry would accept that as an excuse Monday morning? "Look, Jerry," we could say, "we spent Friday trying to breathe some life into this stupid thing, and guess what happened? Our brains rotted out…" No, hmm? Well, we could kidnap the writers and hold them for ransom.'

Cade shook his head. 'They'd just go to the asylum and hire new ones.'

She sighed and lay her head back against the couch. 'Isn't that the truth?' There was a companionable silence, and then she raised her head and gave him a quizzical look. 'Promise not to laugh?' He raised his eyebrows and she shrugged her shoulders. 'I know it sounds crazy, but I'm hungry. You promised you wouldn't laugh!'

'I didn't promise anything,' he said. 'I don't believe you, Padgett. Just a few hours ago, you were going to swear off food for ever.'

'Maybe brain rot affects the stomach. Tell the truth— wouldn't you like something?'

Cade laughed softly. 'It's a miracle you don't weigh two hundred pounds.'

'You can't make me feel guilty, Mr Morgan. It's two a.m. and we've been at this for hours. That's hard work, and hard work burns up lots of calories.' She got to her feet and stretched. 'I can make us some toast.'

'OK, you talked me into it. There must be a Chinese take-away in the neighbourhood. Or a fried chicken place.'

Shannon shook her head. 'They're all closed at this hour. How about some eggs? Do you like yours scrambled or fried?'

'A Morgan Special sounds better,' Cade answered as he followed her into the kitchen. 'Have you got any cheese? Mushrooms would be good, too.'

'I've got something that used to be cheese,' she said, peering into the depths of her almost empty refrigerator. 'What's a Morgan Special?'

She turned as she asked the question. A quick flutter of panic caught in her throat. Cade had come up soundlessly behind her; he was so close that she stumbled against him as she turned. His wool shirt still carried the pleasant scent of the sea, even though the ferry ride was hours past. There was a dark stubble on his jaw; she wondered suddenly what the rasp of his beard would feel like against her skin. Would it be like the touch of his guitar-roughened fingers that had almost driven her insane as they played over her skin during their love scene today?

'On second thoughts,' she said quickly, 'maybe you're right. I do eat too much. I had to lose weight before Jerry would sign me on.'

His eyes flickered over her. 'You look just about perfect to me.'

'Not to the camera,' she said carefully, moving past him. 'It makes everybody look heavier. Besides, I promised you coffee and a rehearsal, and we've had both.'

'I wasn't the one who mentioned something to eat. What's the matter? Are you afraid to try a Morgan Special?'

She swallowed. 'Cade, look . . .'

He grinned at her as he rolled up the sleeves of his shirt. 'Trust me, Padgett. I've smuggled my electric skillet into more hotel rooms than you can shake a stick at. I'll whip the eggs while you grate that cheese. I could use some bacon, if you've got it.'

She sighed and nodded. Trust him? She wasn't even sure she trusted herself any more. Well, at least he hadn't been joking about his cooking ability. His movements were deft as he worked in her tiny kitchen, frying the bacon and whipping the eggs to a froth. Maybe this wasn't such a bad idea at that. Cooking was hardly a romantic pastime; by the time they sat down to eat, surely the sudden tension she felt would have eased.

'I don't suppose you have any wine?' Cade said as he crisped the bacon.

'Sherry,' she answered with an apologetic shrug.

He nodded his approval and took the proffered bottle from her, splashing some of the Harvey's into two jelly glasses and then, with a disarming grin, pouring a generous shot into the beaten eggs.

It was impossible not to return his smile. 'That smells good,' she offered after the eggs had set.

He grinned again. 'It is good,' he said, spooning up a bit and offering it to her. 'Taste.'

Shannon opened her mouth and Cade slipped the spoon between her lips.

'Delicious,' she said.

'Thank you, ma'am. Careful there—don't waste any.' She laughed as he reached out and touched his finger to her lip. 'You missed a bit of bacon,' he began, and suddenly the space between them became charged with electricity. She saw the sudden darkening of his eyes, heard her own uneven breath, felt the rapid thud of her heart. Move away from him, she told herself, but her legs wouldn't obey. If you don't move, if you just stand here and stare at him, he'll put his arms around you and kiss you until escape is no longer possible.

He touched his hand to her cheek. 'Shannon...'

'The toast,' she said thickly.

'Shannon, please...'

'Don't,' she whispered.

'I can read the truth in your eyes,' he said, running his knuckles lightly along her jaw. 'Why do you keep pretending?'

'The toast is burning, Cade. Let me...'

She thought that he wasn't going to let her past him. His eyes were dark slits and a muscle tensed in his cheek. Then he nodded and dropped his hand to his side. She walked to the table and busied herself with buttering the toast and pouring the coffee, until at last she heard him begin to move around the room again. How was she going to get through this? The thought of food made her throat close. But she would eat, at least a little, just enough so Cade would ask her no questions, and they'd have a friendly cup of coffee and then he'd leave and she'd be safe.

'The eggs look great,' she said politely, sitting down opposite him.

His smile was equally polite. 'The coffee's terrific.'

Her hand trembled as she lifted a forkful of omelette. 'This is...is very good,' she said, amazed she'd been able to chew and swallow at all. 'Would you like some toast?'

She lifted the plate and held it out to him. As he reached for it, their fingers touched and the plate slipped free and fell to the table.

'I'm sorry,' she said quickly. 'That was clumsy of me.'

'Shannon...'

'I'll wipe up those crumbs.'

'Damn it, Shannon,' he said roughly. 'You can't keep running away—you're going to have to deal with this sooner or later.'

'I don't know what you're talking about,' she said, shoving back her chair and getting quickly to her feet.

His hand shot out and caught hers as she tried to move past him. 'Yes, you do,' he growled. 'You damned well do.'

'Let go,' she said stiffly.

'You can't keep pretending nothing's happening,' he said, his fingers wrapping tightly around her wrist. 'You've got to face it some time.'

'You'd better leave, Cade,' she said in a breathy voice. 'We had such a nice day together—don't ruin it.'

'Do you feel safer in the make-believe world where emotions are always under control? Is that it?'

'Just listen to you! I hate to spoil your dime-store psychology, but I also refuse to let what we do at work spill into real life.'

His chair squealed in protest as he kicked it back. 'What we feel for each other *is* real life,' he said gruffly, pulling her towards him.

'You're confusing Johnny and Alana with us. I told you, it happens all the time—you just haven't been around the theatre long enough to understand.'

'Then kiss me,' said Cade quickly. 'Kiss me, and then tell me you feel nothing.'

'That's insane.'

'What are you worried about, Padgett? You've been pretty smug about the way you've handled our love scenes.'

'Cade, damn it . . .'

The fingers encircling her wrist tightened as she tried to pull away from him, and the shadow of a smile touched his lips.

'You're right. I'm an amateur when it comes to the theatre. Maybe what happened between us the first time I took you in my arms was a fluke. Maybe you were acting, even then. Hell, you accused me of auditioning for this part by kissing you. Maybe it's the other way around. Maybe you used me to get Crawford to notice you and give you a bigger role.'

'That's the craziest thing I ever heard!' retorted Shannon angrily.

'The more I think about it, the more sense it makes. You were afraid Jerry was going to hand you your walking papers because you weren't carrying your weight with Tony, and then I came along . . .'

'I didn't even know you were going to be on *All Our Tomorrows*,' she sputtered. 'Damn you, Cade, let go of me!'

Cade cocked his head to the side. 'Come on, Padgett. I may be new to the theatre, but I'm not new to show business. Sure, you knew. There must have been a million rumours floating around. Yeah,' he said, 'yeah, it makes sense. You goaded me into kissing you and then you pretended that sudden burst of passion.'

God, she thought, the audacity of the man! He was exactly what she'd thought he was the first time she'd laid eyes on him: six feet two inches of over-inflated celebrity.

'Mr Morgan,' she said carefully, raising her eyes to his, 'I did not goad you into anything.'

'You can admit the truth now, Padgett. You baited me, and then you pretended you felt something when I kissed you.'

The insolent tone of his voice infuriated her as much as his words, and she wrenched herself free of his grasp.

'Pretend? I didn't have to pretend anything, Cade Morgan. You...' The angry accusation caught in her throat as a triumphant grin spread slowly across his face. Shannon flushed and tilted her chin up. 'I didn't mean that the way it sounded.'

Cade nodded. 'Of course,' he said solemnly.

She threw up her hands in exasperation. 'Look, there's no point to this, Cade. Just leave, please.' She started past him, but he moved so rapidly that she was in his arms before there was time to react. 'What...what are you doing? Cade? Cade...?'

He smiled down at her as he threaded one hand in her hair. 'I'm giving you a chance to clarify things,' he said softly, forcing her head back. 'All you have to do is kiss me.'

'I certainly will not kiss you. I...'

'Kiss me and then step back and smile politely and say, what was it you said that first time? That you hadn't been missing much?'

'This is ridiculous.'

'If you can do that, Padgett, I'll leave you alone from now on.'

She stared at him in stony silence. 'Why should I believe you?' she asked finally.

Cade laughed softly. 'You don't really have much choice, Padgett. One way or another, you're going to be kissed. I just thought it might be easier for you if it was without a struggle.'

Look at him, she thought, look at that smug, self-assured expression! He was all the things she'd ever thought and more, and he could kiss her from now until next week and it wouldn't mean a thing. For the life of her, she couldn't figure out why she'd ever thought it had.

'I'm all yours,' she said pleasantly, tilting her head back and closing her eyes. 'Let's just get it over with, OK? Stop that,' she said sharply, as his fingers caressed her cheek. 'You said one kiss.'

'I'm entitled to preliminaries,' he said, his arms tightening around her as she tried to break free of his embrace. 'If you fight me, you're only going to prolong things. That's it,' he murmured as she stood still within his arms. 'Just relax and trust me.'

His words filled her with fury. 'Trust you? Trust you? That's what you always say... You let go of me, Cade Morgan!'

'I told you not to fight me, Shannon,' he said softly, catching her wrists in one hand as she struck out at him. 'Now, you'll have to pay the price of rebellion.'

What was he doing? she thought frantically as he drew her against him. She closed her eyes as she felt the hardness of his body against hers. No, she thought, no... A tremor ran through her as he stroked the long column of her throat. A whisper of anticipation danced along her spine. 'Cade, stop. You said...' Her voice broke as his lips brushed her neck. 'You said one kiss...'

'I've got a confession to make,' he said. 'You're not the only one who's been holding back during our love scenes.'

'I don't know what you mean. I haven't been holding back—there's no reason why I should.'

'If I'd really been making love to you, you couldn't hold back,' he murmured. 'All the techniques in the world wouldn't be enough to save you.'

'I don't know what you're talking about,' she whispered desperately.

He smiled disarmingly. 'Is that so? Do you always babble about laundry when a man is kissing you, Padgett?'

Panic fluttered in her throat. 'That's nonsense, Cade. I...'

'You were lying in my arms this afternoon and suddenly you whispered something about pillowcases.' He chuckled softly. 'You should have know better, Padgett. Wasn't it laundry that got you in trouble the first time?'

A blush spread across her cheeks, but she forced her eyes to meet his. 'I am not going to legitimise this conversation by answering that.'

He leaned towards her until she could feel the warmth of his breath on her face. 'Did you need laundry lists to keep from feeling what I was doing to you?' he whispered. 'To tell you the truth, I was having trouble remembering we weren't alone, myself.'

'Cade, please, this is foolish.'

'But you were right, you know. Hell, I didn't want the world watching us make love.' She made a whimpering sound deep in her throat as his hand slipped under her sweater and she felt the rough warmth of his fingers against her back. 'And here we are, Shannon. No lights, no cameras...'

'Cade,' she whispered. 'Cade...' Remember how angry you are at him, Shannon, she told herself. Remember everything...

But it was too late. She lifted her eyes to his, saw the play of emotions in their indigo depths, and it was as if he had already begun to make love to her. Her breath quickened, and when he smiled, she knew she was lost.

'There's just us,' he murmured thickly. 'Just Cade and Shannon and nobody else...' Her eyes closed as he bent to her and drew her against him. 'Don't be afraid,' he whispered, 'you know it feels right, love.'

Love, he had called her, love, but there was no love between them, there was only this quicksilver excitement that everyone had capitalised on. Love was something that grew slowly and lasted for ever. What they had ignited was passion, the kind that came of the instant intimacy the theatre created. It sold soap and made stars, but it had nothing to do with the real world. How many times had she seen it happen? Hadn't it happened to her?

Maybe not quite like this, she thought, trembling as Cade's mouth touched her closed eyelids. Never like this. She had never felt this driving need deep within her, not just within her body but within her soul, this need to hold and be held, this desire that was more than desire. One kiss, he'd said, one kiss, and then he would stop.

His lips touched hers, softly, tentatively. I can let him do this, she thought, just this, and then I'll say, you see, there was nothing to that, and now you can leave, Cade... One and one are two, two and two are...are... Panic welled within her as his mouth teased hers, urging her to open to him, begging her to withhold nothing. Cade, you promised, you said you'd just, you said you wouldn't . . .

'Don't,' she said, trying to twist her face away from his. 'Please...'

'I love you, Shannon,' he whispered against her mouth. 'Let me show you how much I love you, darling.'

'You don't,' she gasped. 'Cade...'

His hands cupped her face, holding it tightly. 'I know what I feel, Shannon,' he said fiercely.

His mouth closed over hers again, this time with a rough urgency, and suddenly it was impossible to deny what she felt, not to Cade, not to herself. Her mouth softened under his, heating under the sweet fire of his tongue, and she made a sound of soft surrender deep in her throat. Tentatively, her hands moved between them, to spread slowly on his shirt. The rapid thud of his heart was beneath her fingertips, telling her as well as any words ever could that she was not the only one who could no longer control their love scenes. She murmured his name against his lips again and again until it sounded like a litany.

'Yes,' he said, his whisper a fierce song. 'Yes, my love, my own...'

His mouth, his hard, demanding mouth, was stealing her breath away. The earth was tilting under her feet, just as she'd always feared it would if she let him do this. Cade was everything; he was the day and the night and the universe and—oh God, his hand was moving under her sweater, hot against her flesh, his guitar-roughened fingers playing along her ribs.

'Kiss me, Shannon, kiss me, don't hold back, not this time, not tonight, not with me, love, not with me...' She fell back against the wall, her body seared by the heat of his passion. His lips were against her throat, his hands on her skin. 'Let me love you, Shannon,' he whispered. 'Let me, love, let me...'

She gasped as his hands closed over her breasts, the nipples hardening against his palms like the petals of moon flowers closing at the first burning touch of the sun.

'My love,' she sighed, 'my love...'

The admission, so long denied, seemed to free her. Feverishly, she slid her hands under his shirt, her fingers travelling on his skin, through the rough, dark hair that curled upon his chest. Cade drew her to him, his skin silken flame against hers. Together, in a confused tangle of hands and buttons, they pulled off her sweater and corduroy pants.

'Beautiful love,' Cade breathed, 'Goddess of the sea, open your arms, give your love to me...' She thought of all the times she'd heard him sing those opening lines from *Sea Lover,*, yet never with such passion in his voice. 'Beautiful love,' he whispered again, and she lifted her arms to him, but he caught her wrists and brought her hands to her sides. 'Beautiful Shannon,' he sighed, 'my love, my own . . .'

'Cade,' she murmured, 'Cade . . .'

He freed her wrists and shrugged off his shirt. Her hands reached for him, investigating the soft hollows and hard planes of his torso. A feeling of triumph raced through her as he cried out at her touch; there was something primal and exciting about knowing she could do that to him. But the triumph was short-lived; Cade cupped her breasts in his hands and bent to taste her flesh, and it was she who gasped and cried out now. His hands were hot and rough against her skin as he slid the panties from her hips, and then he knelt before her, trailing kisses along the soft inner skin of her thighs.

'So lovely,' he said thickly, 'so lovely . . .'

She cried out as his mouth branded her with his passion. 'I love you, Cade,' she sobbed, and even in the centre of the whirlwind they rode she heard her words and knew they were true, that they would be true even if his were not, but it was too late to talk, too late to think. He was naked against her, his hands cupping her buttocks, lifting her to him. Her legs folded around him and then he was in her and around her, each thrust driving her mind further from her straining body. And just when she thought she would die of a pleasure that transcended any she had ever imagined, she heard the hoarse whisper of her name as he drew her down to the floor and the world exploded around them.

CHAPTER TEN

It was like a child's riddle, Shannon thought, trudging up the stairs to her apartment. What's worse than Friday afternoon traffic in New York? Friday afternoon traffic in New York in the midst of a snowstorm, that's what, although that was stretching things a little. The early December snow had quickly changed from fat, white flakes to a cold, driving rain that had slicked the streets with ice, and every taxi cab in Manhattan had done its usual vanishing act. By the time she had finally caught a bus, she had been wet, chilled and irritable. Only dreams of a hot bath and a hotter cup of tea had got her through the final slippery walk from the bus stop to her apartment.

'Shannon? Good grief, sweetie, hurry up, will you? I am positively freezing my behind off out here!'

Hand on the banister, Shannon paused on the fourth floor landing and stared upward. Her agent stood on the landing above her, wrapped in a fur coat, looking like a large, unkempt animal.

'What are you doing here, Claire?' she asked wearily.

'Waiting for you, obviously. Don't you get any heat in this building? I swear I can feel my feet turning blue,' she wailed, stepping aside as Shannon continued past her.

'Don't tell me,' Shannon said, opening the door to her apartment. 'The heating system died this morning, but Jose promised he'd get it fixed . . . I should have know he wouldn't,' she muttered, walking through the silent rooms, touching her hand to each radiator. 'The first really cold day and the pipes commit suicide. Well, why not?' She shrugged free of her coat and tossed it over the

141

back of a kitchen chair. 'Take that thing off, Claire. You look like a wet teddy bear.'

Claire's eyebrows rose dramatically. 'My, but we're in a good mood, aren't we?'

'I am cold and wet and tired unto death of Alana Dunbar and Jerry Crawford and Rima the Prima. Do you want some tea?'

'Only if you promise not to put rat poison in it,' Claire said mildly, shaking out her wet fur and draping it across the back of a chair.

'Am I that irritable? Sorry. I've been on the go since early morning.'

The agent ran her fingers through her damp hair. 'Busy, busy, busy,' she said. 'That's why I decided to wait for you here. I figured I wouldn't give you another chance to put me off.'

'I haven't. I simply said...'

'I know precisely what you said, Shannon. You said you were busy today and pressed for time yesterday and running late the day before and on your way to a class with Eli the day before that...'

'It's been that kind of week, OK?'

'I decided you'd been avoiding me long enough.'

'Look, I haven't been avoiding you. I...' Shannon took a deep breath and turned to face her agent. 'Let's not argue about it, Claire. Why don't you tell me what's so important that you braved five flights of stairs just to see me? Do you want milk or lemon for your tea?'

'Lemon, sweetie. I'm on a diet. Although I wouldn't mind a cookie or two. Thanks. Would you mind sitting down, please? I hate talking to somebody's back.'

Shannon sighed and slipped into a chair. 'Claire, it's been a long day. Rima was impossible—she had a scene with Cade that had to be finished before he left and she must have blown her lines a billion times. And Jerry snapped at everybody...'

'Our hero left the set early again?'

'What does that mean?' Shannon asked carefully.

Claire shrugged. 'It's just a question, toots. It seems as if the man's been away from the studio more than in it lately.'

'*Tomorrows* has been getting a lot of coverage, that's all.'

The agent smiled. 'Morgan has, you mean. So what was it today?'

'He had a shoot with *People*. They're doing a lead story on him next week.'

'Wonderful,' Claire said pleasantly. 'Let's see, that'll make two, no, three, covers he'll be on all at once. I bet that's some kind of record. *TV Guide* and *Newsweek* and now *People*.'

'I'd think you'd be pleased. It's great publicity for *Tomorrows*.'

'It's good publicity for *Tomorrows*. It's great publicity for Cade Morgan.'

'So?'

'So, what's wrong with sharing some of the spotlight with you? Why doesn't Morgan take you along with him to some of these interviews?'

Shannon lifted her chin. 'Come on, Claire, they're interested in Cade, not me. He's a star.'

'Funny, but there was a time you used to turn that four-letter word into a *real* four-letter word when you said it.'

The kettle shrieked and Shannon shut off the burner. 'I'm too tired to play games, Claire,' she said, pouring the water for their tea. 'What are you getting at?'

'Doesn't it bother you that he's getting all the publicity on *Tomorrows,* sweetie? Especially since you're the reason he's America's primo soap heart-throb.'

'That's not so. Cade turned out to be a good actor.'

'Come on, Shannon. You made him look good, especially at the beginning when he was all nerves.'

'He's not like that any more, Claire. He's been getting terrific reviews . . .'

'Tell me about it,' Claire said sarcastically. 'Which reminds me—*Tomorrows*' ratings went through the roof again this week, did you hear?'

'Yes, so Jerry said. That's good news for all of us, isn't it?'

'Especially Morgan. He's the one who's reaping all the publicity. Seems to me he'd be willing to share a little of it with you.'

Shannon wrapped her hands around her mugful of tea, letting the warmth seep through her. 'I'm getting publicity. *TV Guide* interviewed me, didn't they?'

'They'll give you a paragraph, if you're lucky.' Claire pursed her lips thoughtfully. 'Now, if Morgan introduced you to people, you know, if he showed them that the chemistry on-screen carries over off-screen . . .'

Dark patches of crimson rose to Shannon's cheeks. 'Forget it.'

'Well, that's why Crawford matched you two up in the first place, remember? God, they'd eat it up! They'd . . .'

'Stop it, Claire.'

'Come on, Shannon, you can't fool me. I've seen the way you look at him. Maybe you can pull the wool over everybody else's eyes, but this is good old Claire, remember? You don't have to pretend with me.'

'I know you mean well,' Shannon said slowly, putting the mug down on the counter. 'But . . .'

'I'm trying to get some mileage out of all this for you, sweetie. But I can't boost your career unless you help.'

'I'm not going to use my private life that way.'

'Hey, I'm not asking you to invite anybody into your bedroom. I'm simply suggesting you make the most of an opportunity. I'm just suggesting what Morgan should have . . .'

'Did you want to see me for anything else?' Shannon asked coldly. 'If not, I've got things to do.'

The agent sighed. 'OK, OK, take it easy. What I really want to settle is what comes next. This stint on *Tomorrows* won't last for ever, toots.'

'It's only December. You said this would go four months.'

'Well, sure, I hope it will. But you've got to make plans for later—you know, trade on what little name recognition you've gotten. I told you I've had feelers from Rob Michaels about that revival of *Joe Egg* he's doing in LA in May. And Papp's talking about *Twelfth Night* for Shakespeare in the Park this summer. I can't put these guys off for ever, kid. You've got to make some decisions while they still know who you are.'

'I know, I know. I told you, I will.'

'Yeah, but when, sweetie? You know what this business is like. Today you're hot, tomorrow you're not. Once you and *Tomorrows* part company, we'll be back to "Shannon Who?" That's why you're nuts to be so stubborn about this Cade Morgan thing. Let them know who you are.'

'Goodbye, Claire,' Shannon said firmly, shoving her agent's still damp coat at her and leading her to the door. 'I'd appreciate it if you'd call before you drop by in the future.'

'Go on, get as huffy as you like. I'm still gonna tell you what's on my mind. What's good for you is good for me, but, I mean, if you don't take my advice... Just think about it, OK? You've got an opportunity, use it. Morgan sure is. The word around town is that his agent's been out there shaking hands and slapping backs and doing everything but hiring a skywriter.'

'Goodbye, Claire,' Shannon repeated. 'I'll call you tomorrow.'

'At least decide what you want me to tell Michaels. I have to tell him something.'

The slam of the door cut off Claire's complaints. Shannon let out her breath and leaned against the wall, waiting until she heard the sharp sound of her agent's heels tapping down the hall. Lord, the woman was persistent! And she meant well—but not all the good intentions in the world would make her trade on what she and Cade felt for each other. It was intense, it was wonderful—and it was private.

Perhaps it had something to do with the way they'd met or with the millions who watched their on-screen love scenes, but from the beginning, they had kept their love affair quiet. And becoming lovers had changed the way they approached their scenes together. Alana Dunbar and Johnny Wolff met before the cameras now, not Shannon and Cade. The love scenes still 'sizzled'—they were both good actors. Besides, the sparks they struck would always be there, no matter how professional they were. But the real Shannon and Cade embraced only when they were alone—and they were alone as often as possible.

Shannon kicked off her shoes and padded across the room. Her apartment felt like a refrigerator. She touched the living-room radiator and sighed. Still cold. The one in the bedroom was the same, although it gave a strangled gurgle when she banged it with her hand. The thing to do was get out of her damp clothing and into something warm, and then go back and finish her tea. She hit the playback button on her telephone answering machine and then pulled her dress over her head. The machine whirred into life and Claire's voice filled the bedroom.

'Hi, there, sweetie. Do me a favour and call me when you get in, OK? I . . .'

Shannon tossed the dress aside and pressed the button again.

'Uh, this is Jose. The superintendent? Uh, I need to get into your apartment tomorrow, OK? To work on your pipes, right? So maybe you could drop off your keys...'

I'll be dead from the cold by tomorrow, she thought, hitting the button on the answering machine. Quickly, she pulled on a pair of baggy grey sweatpants, a navy sweatshirt, and a Ragg sweater, listening while the machine clicked, whirred and returned to record. Her feet felt like lumps of ice and she put on white wool socks and then added her Mickey Mouse slippers. The glamorous Shannon Padgett, relaxing at home, she thought, grinning at her reflection in the mirror.

She glanced at the clock as she padded into the kitchen. Cade would probably be calling soon. He'd said he'd get in touch first chance he had. Picking up her teacup, she sipped at the liquid, made a face and tossed the tepid stuff into the sink. What was the point of making tea and drinking it cold? She sighed as she refilled the kettle and set it on the range. Darn Claire, anyway! Why couldn't she simply be glad that *All Our Tomorrows* was doing as well as it was?

Be fair, she told herself as she took a box of tea-bags from the shelf. Claire had been a pest lately, but she was only trying to do her job. Even without the kind of media attention Claire wanted, Shannon's career was on the move. There were doors opening to her now that had been closed before, and all her agent was trying to tell her was what she already knew. Either you stepped through those doors quickly or they swung shut. Nothing in the theatre was deader than yesterday's hit.

The kettle shrilled and she shut off the burner. No, you couldn't blame Claire for wanting to make the most of what was happening. It was just that nothing—not even the New York offer or the Los Angeles offer—was as important as Cade.

She stirred a spoonful of sugar into her tea, watching as the amber liquid swirled and eddied. Still, she had to deal with those offers and she had to do it soon. You could only put off people like Papp and Michaels just so long. How strange life was, she thought, sipping the hot tea. If the offers had come just a couple of weeks ago, she'd have been on the phone with Claire ten times a day,

luxuriating in the pleasure of deciding which of them to
accept. Not that it wasn't still exciting. It was just that she
didn't want to tie herself to three months in Los Angeles
next summer or two months here in New York or anywhere else, not now. She wanted to be with Cade, and he
wanted to be with her, and that was all that mattered.

'There's a little bistro in Marseilles that you'd love,'
he'd said as they had dined in a restaurant overlooking
the East River. 'It's a madhouse during the summer, but
it's peaceful and quiet in the spring.' And the other
afternoon, reading lines together, he'd suddenly looked
up and smiled at her. 'Jack and Phil are going to open a
place in Seattle next fall, did I tell you?' And she'd said
no, he hadn't, and he'd smiled again. 'Seattle's a terrific
city,' he'd said. 'You'd like it.' And then, just last night,
as they returned to her apartment after dinner, a couple
of stoned kids had brushed by, muttering something
vaguely obscene, and Cade had tensed. 'We've got to get
you out of this neighbourhood,' he'd said. 'It's too
damned dangerous.'

The sudden cry of the telephone startled her. She was
half-way out of her chair before she remembered that the
answering machine was still on. Perhaps that was just as
well; Claire might have decided to try another approach.
It wasn't until she was rinsing out her teacup that it suddenly occured to her that it might be Cade calling. Stupid, she thought, wiping her hands on her sweatpants and
hurrying out of the kitchen. Stupid . . .

Damn! Of course, it was Cade. The machine whirred
and clicked and then his husky voice reached out to her
through the silent rooms.

'Hello, love. I called the studio but they said you'd
gone for the day. I'm going to be stuck here for a while.
Do you want to meet me at Nico's at eight or shall I come
by to your apartment for you? Call me at 555-4180 and
let me know . . .'

'Yes,' she gasped, snatching up the telephone and slamming the disconnect switch on the answering machine.

Cade laughed softly. 'A machine that responds, hmm? That's wonderful. But it has to learn to make choices.'

'Yes, I'll meet you at Nico's and yes, I'll wait here for you,' she said breathlessly, sinking down on the bed. 'Whichever you prefer.'

'You're a nice, obliging sort, Padgett. Has anybody ever told you that before?'

'Not lately,' she said, thinking of Claire and the argument they'd just had. 'How was your day?'

Cade sighed. 'Long and dull. And yours?'

'Short and dull,' she laughed, sitting down on the bed. 'The weather put Jerry into a panic—I think he's driving to Connecticut for the weekend—so he called things to a close a couple of hours ahead of time, which was just as well, because it took me for ever to get home. I didn't really do much after you left the studio this morning, anyway. Jerry spent a lot of time doing camera angles on Rima. She was purring like a cat with a dish of cream.'

'Good old Rima. Well, at least you had an easy day.'

Shannon settled back against the pillows and smiled. 'Am I supposed to gather from your tone that posing for *People* was difficult?'

Cade chuckled softly. 'It was hell, Padgett. I'll expect you to treat this old man very kindly tonight.'

'Oh, I will, Mr Morgan, sir. Milk toast, and tea, and . . .'

'That's not quite what I had in mind. I was thinking more of something soothing to the body and spirit. A quiet dinner at Nico's and later, back to your apartment for some much needed rest.'

'That's what I'm doing right now,' Shannon said primly. 'Resting in bed after a hard day's work.'

Cade's voice dropped to a husky whisper. 'What are you wearing, Padgett? That blue teddy with the lace straps?'

Shannon looked down at her sweater-topped sweatsuit and her Mickey Mouse feet and grinned.

'Nope. Try again.'

'A black satin négligé?'

'Uh-uh. Something even sexier.'

Cade laughed softly. 'Don't tell me—you've got your mouse feet on.'

'Ah yes, Mr Morgan. The feet that drive men wild.'

'I can't take much more of this,' he growled. 'I'll be right over.'

'Better bring your thermals,' she said. 'This place is as cold as Alana Dunbar's heart. The heating system's dead.'

Cade's chuckle was soft and wicked. 'I can be there in twenty minutes with a sure cure for chilblains.'

'I thought you had to work late.'

'There's no sacrifice too great. Your health is my first concern.'

'How noble,' she laughed. 'Well, how did it feel to be photographed by *People*? Even Rima was impressed.'

'I don't want to sound immodest, young woman, but you forget, I was a *People* cover before. I won three Grammys two years ago.'

Shannon sighed. 'That's disgusting! Two covers in two years? For shame, Cade Morgan. How can you live with yourself?'

'It's not easy,' he chuckled. 'Listen, I'm going to have to go in a couple of minutes. Tell you what—meet me at Nico's at eight. We'll have an early dinner and then take in that Tracy-Hepburn revival in the Village.'

Shannon curled the telephone cord around her wrist. 'I thought you wanted to do that tomorrow night.'

There was a brief pause and then Cade cleared his throat. 'Bad news, sweetheart. I was going to tell you during dinner... I won't be here tomorrow night.'

'Won't be here?' she asked, swinging her feet to the floor. 'What do you mean?'

'I'm flying to Los Angeles early in the morning. Shannon. I'll be gone all weekend.'

'All weekend?' she repeated. 'But you didn't say anything...'

'I didn't know about it until this afternoon. My manager went out to California to make arrangements for a farewell concert for the Marauders at the Hollywood Bowl next year...'

'And he needs you there,' she said slowly, thinking of the long, lonely hours stretching ahead.

'Yeah. Well, no, not for that. He called me this afternoon—seems he went to a party last night and met the guy who just took over Scorpio Studios. The bottom line is that Scorpio's going to do a film in LA in May and they may have a part for me.'

'That's wonderful,' she said happily. Los Angeles in May, hmm? The offer from Rob Michaels was for Los Angeles in May. Thank you, Claire, she thought.

'Hank—my manager—wants me to meet this guy before Scorpio makes any casting decisions. I think it's a long shot, but...'

'Oh, you should meet him, Cade,' she said, lying back on the bed, thinking that she'd save the news about the *Joe Egg* offer she'd had until Cade had actually been offered the part in the film. Not that she had any doubts about it. He'd work for Scorpio and she'd work for Rob Michaels and they'd be together. 'It sounds like a great opportunity.'

'Well, that's what Hank says.' He laughed softly. 'You sound as if you'll be glad to get rid of me for the weekend, Padgett. Won't you miss me at all?'

She smiled into the telephone. 'Maybe,' she teased. 'Then again, maybe not.'

'You'd damn well better miss me, woman! And you'd better be prepared to show how much you did when I get back.'

'I'll try and think of something,' she said. 'When will you be back?'

'Monday night, the latest.'

'You mean, you won't be at the studio Monday?' Shannon chuckled. 'Jerry's going to love that. He moaned all afternoon about having to shoot around you today.'

'Well, he's just going to have to live through it. Nobody's indispensable.'

'Cade Morgan is,' she laughed. 'After all, more people are buying *Glimmer* toothpaste and *Speedo* detergent. And *Tomorrows'* ratings are up.'

'That still doesn't make me indispensable, Shannon.'

'But Mr Morgan,' she said teasingly, 'you're the heart throb of millions of women. Don't you understand?'

'*All Our Tomorrows* was there long before I joined it. It'll be there long after I'm gone.'

She sighed dramatically. 'Ah, what an innocent you are! When you leave, *Tomorrows* will slip into oblivion.'

'Do me a favour, Shannon,' Cade said sharply. 'Don't sound like Crawford's stooge.'

'Hey,' she said softly, 'don't get so upset, Morgan. I was just teasing you.'

Cade let out his breath. 'I'm sorry, love. I guess I'm more tired than I realised. It's just that Crawford's always trying to make me feel . . . Look, nothing is for ever. Things change, you know? You can't freeze time.'

He sounded tired, she thought. You could joke about magazine covers all you liked, but a picture session wasn't easy. She could still remember the modelling she'd done when she first came to New York and how tiring it was.

'The only thing freezing right now is me,' she said lightly. 'I'll meet you at Nico's, OK?'

'OK,' he said finally. 'And then we'll see that film.'

'And then you'll give me something to remember you by,' Shannon said softly. 'It's going to be a long, lonely weekend.'

CHAPTER ELEVEN

'I HATE Mondays,' Jerry Crawford snarled. 'And this is the worst one in the history of this damned soap.'

His words rolled over the quiet studio from the control booth. Shannon looked into the darkness beyond the set and swallowed.

'I . . . I'm sorry, Jerry,' she called. 'Did I get that take wrong again?'

'She looks awful, Make-up,' the director said, ignoring her. 'Get in here and do something about the colour of her face, will you? What did you do? Spend the weekend in Bermuda?'

'No, no, I didn't,' she said nervously. 'In fact, the pipes broke in my apartment, and I spent the weekend . . .'

'That was a rhetorical question, Miss Padgett. Frankly, I don't care if you spent in it Timbuctoo.' The control room door slammed and Jerry stalked on to the set, Rima the Prima by his side. 'Make-up, I want Padgett to look as if she has a glow of excitement, not a goddamned fever, understand?'

'Sure, Jerry,' the make-up man said. He rolled his eyes and gave Shannon a sympathetic smile as he scurried towards her. 'No problem.' He turned her face to the light and began dusting her cheeks with powder. 'Don't let him get to you,' he whispered. 'Some Mondays are worse than others.'

'He's never been this bad before,' she murmured.

The make-up man nodded. 'I think he's annoyed because Morgan's not here. I heard him muttering something to Rima.'

'But Cade didn't have any scenes today.' She closed her eyes as the powder puff moved lightly across her forehead. 'What's the difference?'

'All I know is what I heard, dear. The man was going on about Morgan being self-interested...tilt your chin up a bit, will you?'

'Rima's the one who's selfish,' she said, doing as he'd asked. 'Crawford changed her lines three times this morning, just to suit her. And meanwhile he's done nothing but bark at me. And Rima loves every minute of it. She keeps looking at me with that smug smile on her face.'

'Yes, I noticed. Well, just tune out.'

'I wish I could, but...' Shannon raised her hand to her cheek and touched it lightly. 'Is my face really red?'

'Your cheeks are kind of ruddy, yes, but don't worry about it. I'll bring the colour down.'

'I hope I'm wrong,' she said slowly, 'but I just realised...Is this a bump, Arnie? Next to my nose?' She closed her eyes and shook her head. 'Tell me it isn't.'

'Listen, if you're talking about an allergy attack, forget it,' the make-up man hissed. 'Crawford will skin us both.'

'My God, I can feel it happening. My skin is beginning to tingle... It's his fault, anyway. How much of this glop can you put on somebody's face? First my cheekbones were too high, then they were too flat. My eye liner was too dark when we started and then it was too light...'

'Be sure and tell him that,' Arnie muttered. 'Are you kidding? It's going to be your fault—and mine, of course. Can't you do something?'

'I have some antihistamine tablets in my dressing-room. Maybe he'll call a break. If I take the tablets fast enough...'

'Make-up, what the hell's taking so long?'

'I'm almost done, Jerry.' Arnie ran his finger along Shannon's forehead. 'I hate to tell you this,' he whispered frantically, 'but you're getting pinker by the second and you've got some little spots up here... Boy, in another five minutes, you're probably going to look like a lobster.'

'Bite your tongue,' she said, choking back a nervous laugh. 'I'm allergic to shellfish, too. All right, all right, don't look at me that way. I'll find a way to get through this next scene in one take and then I'll get some antihistamine. Jerry will never know anything's wrong.'

'One take?' The make-up man jerked his head towards the side of the set. 'Rima's in this scene, remember? It'll take a dozen shots to get this one in the can. In fact, considering Crawford's mood, you'll be lucky to be done by nightfall.'

Shannon's glance skittered past Arnie's shoulder and her eyes met Rima's coolly amused gaze. 'Well, then, I'll ask for a break. I'll say I've got to go to the john or something.'

'Aren't you done yet, Make-up?' Jerry asked irritably.

'Yes, yes, all finished. There we go.'

Jerry scowled as the man scuttled off to the side and then he motioned Rima forward. 'Rima, dear, this is a pivotal scene,' he said pleasantly, slipping an arm around her shoulders. 'I want the audience to empathise with you. As for you, Padgett,' he said, glaring at Shannon, 'you've just been told your father left you controlling interest in the company Rima thought was hers and you can't wait to rub it under her nose. Your stepmother's never been your favourite person and this is the chance you've been waiting for. Try and look alive, please. You were as exciting as my Great-Aunt Tillie during the run-through.'

Just look at that, Shannon thought, staring at Jerry as he stood with his arm around Rima. When did she become his favourite person? What's going on here? Have I missed something?

'I'll do my best,' she said carefully, touching her index finger to her cheek. Her face felt as if it were on fire. She cleared her throat and forced her lips back from her teeth in what she hoped was a smile. 'Er—Jerry, I was just wondering—were you planning on calling a break soon?'

There was a thick silence. 'No, I was not, Miss Padgett,' the director said with forced cordiality. 'But I gather you were hoping I was.'

Shannon nodded. 'Yes,' she said brightly, 'I was. I—er—I need a couple of minutes. I have to...'

'Don't tell me your troubles,' he snapped. 'I've got enough of my own.'

'I—er—I'm sure you do, Jerry...'

'"I'm sure you do, Jerry",' he mimicked. 'You're in an amazingly good mood, all things considered.'

Lord, she thought, now he's angry because he thinks I'm not taking him seriously. 'Look, Jerry—er—Mr Crawford, I know you're not pleased with the way things are going this morning. Believe me, I wouldn't ask for a break if I didn't really need one.'

Crawford threw his hands up in disgust. 'Skip the speech, OK? All right, everybody, take ten.'

'Thanks, Mr Crawford. I...'

'Ten minutes, Padgett, and then you'd better be ready or I'll tell the writers to arrange Alana Dunbar's fatal accident ahead of time.'

An embarrassed silence fell over the technicians and crew as the director turned and stalked off the set. 'Well,' the Make-up man said finally, 'anybody for a quick coffee?'

'Great idea,' somebody said quickly.

'Yeah, terrific...'

Within seconds, the set was deserted. Shannon blinked back a sudden welling of tears as she started slowly towards the shadowed perimeter.

'It isn't your fault,' a breathy voice said from the darkness. 'Don't let him upset you.'

'Who's there? Rima, is that you?' Shannon asked. She frowned and rubbed her hand across her eyes as Rima stepped into the light. 'I didn't know anyone was still here.'

Rima held out a packet of Kleenex. 'Here,' she said pleasantly, 'you look as if you need a tissue.'

Shannon looked at the older woman suspiciously and then she nodded.

'Thanks,' she said. 'That's very kind.'

Rima smiled and tilted her head to the side. 'Rough day, hmm?'

'Yes, I guess you could say that. Jerry—Mr Crawford . . . he's been furious with me all morning.'

Rima nodded. 'Such a pity,' she said sweetly. Shannon looked up sharply, but Rima's face was a study in innocence. 'I thought we could run through our little scene,' she said. 'See if we can get something extra into it.'

Three months, Shannon thought, staring at the other woman, three months of working together and she's never said more than a half-dozen words to me until now.

'That's a good idea,' she said finally. 'But why? I mean, you've never wanted to before.'

'Well, this is such an important few pages, Sharon. What happens in this scene lays the groundwork for the new story line.'

'Shannon,' Shannon said automatically. 'My name is Shannon.'

'Sorry.'

'That's all right, Rima. Well, sure, it's fine with me if you want to do a reading. But I think you're wrong about this scene—it doesn't set up anything new.'

'But it does. The writers are going to focus on my attempts to regain control of my dead husband's fortune.'

'The legal battle between Alana and her stepmother, you mean. That's not new.'

'The legal thing's out, Shanna.'

'It's Shannon, Rima. What do you mean, it's out? Jerry said we were going to do some exterior shots outside a courthouse in Westchester.'

The other woman shrugged her narrow shoulders. 'You couldn't very well expect them to stick with the same storyline, not now that Cade's...' She hesitated and turned away, but not before Shannon saw a triumphant flash in the emerald green eyes. A warning tingle crawled up her spine.

'Now that Cade's what?'

'Never mind, Shanna. I'm sure you don't want to discuss it.'

'Discuss what? I don't know what you're talking about.'

Rima shrugged her shoulders. 'I don't blame you for taking that attitude,' she purred. 'It's such a difficult thing to have happen, isn't it? Professionally as well as personally. I must say, I agree with Jerry. You're taking it rather well.'

Shannon moved a step closer. 'Listen, I don't know what you're talking about ...'

'Of course you don't,' Rima said soothingly. 'Not that there's much you can do about it, of course.'

'My God, will you stop beating around the bush? What are you talking about, Rima? Is my character going to fade? Is that it?'

The woman turned towards Shannon, a thin smile on her face. 'That's certainly one way of putting it, Sheena.'

Shannon's eyes narrowed. 'My name is Shannon,' she said carefully. 'That's not so difficult to remember. I'm sure you can get it straight just once if you really put some effort into it.'

'Temper, temper!' Rima's smile faded and her mouth narrowed into a cold line. 'Better remember that it isn't

the same without the big star around to protect you. No
more delicate treatment from Jerry, no more great camera angles...'

'What are you talking about?'

'...no more juicy scenes.'

Shannon's face felt as if someone had set it ablaze. She
raised her hand to her cheek, almost wincing at the heat
that blazed against the coolness of her palm.

'Listen,' she said carefully, 'when you get ready to talk
sense, look me up. Until then, I'll be in my dressing-
room.'

'I don't blame you for trying to put up a good front,'
Rima said soothingly. 'It must be terrible to find out that
your relationship with Morgan wasn't all you thought,
hmm?'

Shannon had started across the studio, but she paused
as Rima's words fell around her like shards of glass. 'And
what, exactly, does that mean?' she asked quietly, turning back to the set.

Rima tossed her head. 'Come on, Sheila. Do you think
people are blind? I know you and Morgan were *très* dis-
creet, but—look, you played your cards and you lost.
Who'd have dreamed our sexy hero would decide to leave
Tomorrows so suddenly?'

'Are you crazy?' Shannon shook her head in disbelief. 'Boy, this place is a madhouse. Cade's not leaving
Tomorrows.'

'Look, Shelley...'

'Shannon,' Shannon said through her teeth.
'S H A N N...'

'Yes, sorry. Look, don't let it out on me. It's not my
fault your boyfriend left us for Hollywood. I guess when
the movies beckon, everything else falls by the wayside.
I told Jerry I'd do whatever I could for the show, of
course. That's why I wanted to talk to you about our next
scene.'

A giddy sense of relief swept through Shannon and she laughed aloud. 'Is that what this is all about? Listen, somebody got their signals crossed. I hate to put the kiss of death on such a wonderful rumour, but . . . Cade's in Hollywood, yes, but he's there to talk about a picture deal for next spring.'

'Do tell,' Rima said sweetly, her emerald eyes bright with malice.

'God, you're incredible. How could you think Cade would walk out on all of us?'

'How could he walk out on you, Sherry, isn't that the real question? Well, I guess only you would know the answer to that one. All I know is that his agent called Jerry last night and told him that Cade wouldn't be back.'

'What? You must be crazy!'

'*Jerry* was crazy,' Rima laughed. 'But I told him, look on the bright side of things. That's the great thing about this type of TV drama—there are always at least half a dozen continuing plot-lines and one can always get rid of a character, poof, with just the stroke of a typewriter key! And I said, Jerry, I said, isn't it terrific that the writers always come up with something creative when the pressure's on? Johnny's and Alana's sudden deaths will be a great intro for the new incest angle they've been thinking about for me.' Rima frowned and leaned forward. 'What is that on your cheek, Shari, that red spot?'

'Nothing,' Shannon said quickly, putting her hand to her cheek. 'It's just a blotch. Did Jerry tell you all this?'

'Are you coming down with something, Shirley?' The famous green eyes narrowed as she peered at Shannon. 'You have these little red spots all over your face.'

'No, no, it's nothing, Rima. Just a little allergic reaction. Answer my question. When did Jerry . . .'

'You're sick,' Rima said, her voice rising as she backed away. 'What is it, the measles or something? Jerry, where are you? Look, I'm not playing this scene, not with what's-her-name coming down with God knows what.'

'Coming down with what?' The director moved into the light and peered at Shannon as if she were a laboratory specimen. 'Jeez, Padgett, what the hell's happened to you?'

'It's nothing,' Shannon insisted, putting her hand to her face. 'I have some pills in my dressing-room.' She took a deep breath and stepped closer to him. 'Jerry, please, I . . . I have to talk to you.'

'Listen, we've gone past ten minutes here.'

'Jerry . . . Mr Crawford, please—it's about Cade.'

Crawford hesitated and then took her arm. 'All right, let's go get your pills, Padgett. What the hell, we can't tape with you looking like a pizza.' He glanced down at her and then cleared his throat. 'Look,' he added gruffly, 'I shouldn't have been quite that hard on you this morning.'

'That's all right,' she said quickly. 'I just want to know about Cade . . .'

'Hell, I can't hold you responsible for your boyfriend.' The director forced a smile to his face as they walked through the studio. 'Guilt by association is frowned on in polite society.'

When they finally stepped into her dressing-room, Shannon closed the door and leaned against it. 'Jerry, please . . .' She heard the quaver in her voice and she took a deep breath. Get hold of yourself, she thought. Don't fall apart. 'Jerry, you and Rima both seem to think I know what's going on here, but I don't. I wish somebody would tell me what's happening.'

Crawford scowled. 'Am I supposed to believe that you're not party to all this, Padgett?'

'Party to what?' she managed to whisper.

'You and Morgan were seeing each other, weren't you?' he demanded.

Shannon opened her mouth and closed it again. 'Yes,' she said finally. 'Yes...'

The director shrugged. 'Then you know he's gone to California.'

She nodded, tempted for a second to laugh and tell him, as she'd told Rima, that the rumour mill had gone wild, but something in his face stopped her. 'Yes, of course, I know,' she said slowly, sitting down at her dressing-table. 'He went out for the weekend, on business, and he'll be back tonight.'

Her heart kicked against her ribs as she saw the look of sudden pity in Jerry's eyes. 'Jeez,' he said softly, 'you really don't know, do you?'

'Don't know what?' she asked. 'Please, Jerry...'

'Morgan's not coming back tonight, Shannon. He's not coming back at all, except to do a couple of days' work that I all but bludgeoned him into.'

Shannon looked at him in disbelief. 'What are you talking about?' she murmured. 'Of course he's coming back. He told me...'

'Our big star's signed a contract to do a movie for Scorpio Studios.'

'In the spring, Jerry. In May.'

'Morgan's signed to do a film right now. They start shooting a week from Wednesday in Tahiti. They'll be there for the next three months at least.'

Shannon shook her head. 'That's impossible,' she said positively. 'Someone's made a mistake.'

The director shifted his weight from one foot to the other. 'Listen, I think you'd better take those pills. You don't look so hot.' She looked at him blankly. 'Shannon, please—we've got to tape a scene.' Automatically, she fished in her pocketbook until she found the anti-histamine tablets and popped two into her mouth. 'Thanks,' Crawford said with a quick smile. 'I guess you're not much in the mood for it, but...'

'Look, Jerry, I know there's a reasonable explanation for all this. There has to be. Cade wouldn't . . . I mean, I know him. I . . .'

Crawford cleared his throat and patted her shoulder clumsily. 'Damn it, Padgett, I thought for sure you knew. I wish I'd spoken to your agent first. I tried to. I called her office this morning and left a message, but . . . I'm really sorry. I mean, along with everything else, I hate to dump this on you, too, but . . . *All Our Tomorrows* has to keep going. I've got no choice about the storyline. You see that, don't you?'

'You're changing it,' she said flatly, and Jerry nodded.

'I have to. Without Morgan, I've got to kill you off. You understand.'

Shannon raised her eyes and looked at the director's reflection in the dressing-table mirror. You're an actress, she told herself, reading the wary concern in the man's eyes. You play the part through to the final curtain.

'Yes, of course,' she said evenly. 'Alana's nothing without Johnny.'

'I'm glad you're taking it so well, Padgett,' Crawford said. 'And listen, I really am sorry about this morning.'

'Don't worry about it,' she said, forcing a smile to her lips. My God, she thought, catching a glimpse of herself in the mirror, was that pasty face hers?

'Are you OK? You look awfully pale.'

'I'm fine,' she lied. 'It's just the pills doing their job.'

'Are you sure? You don't look so good.'

'Really, I'm OK. Do you want to get to the taping now?'

There was a light tap at the door. It swung open and Claire stepped into the tiny room. Her glance swept past Jerry and fell on Shannon.

'Well,' she said brightly, 'I see I'm just in time for the first meeting of the *Tomorrows'* chapter of the Cade

Morgan Fan Club.' She smiled and put her hand on Shannon's shoulder. 'How are you doing, sweetie?'

'I'm fine,' she murmured, putting her hand over her agent's and clasping it tightly.

'Five minutes, OK?' Jerry asked. 'Maybe we can get this scene squared away fast and we can all get the hell out of here.'

Shannon nodded, the smile still plastered to her face. As soon as the door swung shut, she closed her eyes and bowed her head.

'You know?' she asked, and Claire nodded.

'Crawford left a message with my secretary. I'm sorry, toots.'

'Damn it, I don't want to hear any more sympathy messages!' Shannon said angrily, slamming her hand down on the dressing-table. 'Look, there's got to be a perfectly reasonable explanation for all this. I'll bet anything it's a mistake. Cade went out there at the last minute, Claire. He didn't even really want to go—it was just to meet somebody and talk about some movie they're making next spring.'

Claire's hand tightened on Shannon's shoulder. 'Listen, sweetie, I'd love to tell you what you want to hear, but I can't. Crawford's office gave me all the gory details and I confirmed them.'

'But ... but ... it hasn't been four months yet,' Shannon said, grasping at straws. 'Remember? You said these parts would run four months.'

'Morgan wouldn't sign anything more than a month-to-month contract, and he insisted on a rider that would permit him to cancel with one week's notice. I thought it was because he wanted to negotiate for more bucks, but this morning I heard that he'd already talked to Scorpio Studios a few months ago about this movie. They didn't want him—Hollywood's run by a bunch of bankers. What do they know from musicians? "Show us you can act," the grey flannel suits said, "and we'll talk it over."

So Mr Morgan got himself a part on *Tomorrows* and did just that.'

Shannon took a deep breath. 'Claire... Are you saying that Cade planned this?'

The agent shrugged her shoulders. 'I'm saying he put his money on a horse that was a sure thing. The worst that could have happened was exposure on *Tomorrows*. The best was that he'd have this Hollywood contract in his pocket.'

'But I spoke to him yesterday morning, for God's sake! He phoned me from LA—he said the smog was awful and the traffic was worse than New York's.'

'They signed him yesterday afternoon, kid.' Claire glanced down at her client's face and cleared her throat. 'Look, let me speak to Crawford. The hell with this "the show must go on" garbage. You've put in a long day and ...'

Shannon got to her feet and shook her head. 'It isn't necessary,' she said firmly. 'Besides, I know all this is some sort of terrible error.'

'Shannon, sweetie...'

'You'll see,' she repeated as stubbornly as a child determined to go on believing in Santa Claus. 'He'd never lie to me. Not Cade.'

She strode briskly back on to the set, ignoring Rima's sly glances and pretending not to notice Jerry's sympathetic ones. It took an hour to tape her brief scene with Rima, but finally it was over. By the time she and Claire reached Shannon's apartment, she was half convinced Cade would be waiting outside the door, ready to take her in his arms.

But the stairs and the hallway were empty and quiet; not even a telegram awaited her. Claire reached out and touched Shannon's shoulder as they stepped into the apartment.

'Listen, toots, it's freezing in this place.'

Shannon nodded. 'Yes, I know. The heat's not working.'

'So throw some stuff together and come bunk with me,' Claire said briskly. 'We'll do our nails and our hair and have girl-type fun together...'

But Shannon had already switched on her answering machine. Claire's words faded into silence as Cade's familiar voice spoke.

'Shannon?' he said, and then there was a pause. 'I'm sorry,' he murmured at last. 'I wanted to tell you the news myself. It would have been better that way...'

Then, at last, Shannon knew that everyone had been telling her the truth. Cade was gone. A lancet of pain sliced into her heart. She snatched the machine from the table and hurled it across the room, killing Cade in a jumble of broken plastic and unwound tape. And then the reality of it all swept over her, and she buried her face in her hands.

'Oh, God,' she whispered, 'I want to die...'

Claire bent down and put her arms around her. 'No way, sweetie,' she said grimly, 'It's bad enough the son of a bitch killed Alana Dunbar. I absolutely refuse to let him take Shannon Padgett down the tubes, too.'

CHAPTER TWELVE

'You'd think I'd remember whether you take cream in your coffee after three days, wouldn't you?' Claire asked, smiling as she padded into the dining alcove of her townhouse. 'My head's like a sieve.'

'Black, thanks,' Shannon answered. 'Which reminds me—I stopped by at my apartment yesterday afternoon. Jose thinks the heating system will be fixed some time today. I should be able to move back home this evening.'

'For goodness' sake, I didn't mean to suggest it was time you left. Matter of fact, it's been fun having you here.' Claire grinned as she spread marmalade on a piece of buttered toast. 'I haven't had a roomie since my college days, and you're lots more fun than she was.'

Shannon's eyebrows arched above the rim of her cup. 'Fun?' she said, lowering the cup to the table. 'There must be a word that describes the way I've been since Monday, but I'd bet my last cent that it wouldn't be "fun".'

Claire sighed and bit into her toast. 'You wouldn't say that if you'd known my room-mate.' She munched in thoughtful silence and then swallowed. 'You are one tough lady. Even Crawford's impressed. He says you've been working your tail off, running rings around Rima and everybody else.'

'Hard work is good for you,' Shannon said blithely. 'Didn't anybody ever tell you that?'

'They also told me you can't put in twelve hour days if you pace the floor all night. Something's gotta give, sooner or later.'

'I'm not worried about it,' Shannon said with a smile. 'This is still "sooner".' The smile faded and she covered Claire's hand with her own. 'I've got to keep busy, Claire. Otherwise . . . I've just got to.'

'Yeah, I understand. Er—have you replaced your answering machine yet?'

Shannon drew her hand back and lifted her cup to her lips again. 'What for?' she asked carefully. 'After all, you're my agent. You handle all my business calls. I never really needed that thing in the first place.'

The agent took a deep breath. 'Listen, sweetie,' she said slowly, 'you've got to talk to Morgan eventually.'

'I don't see why.'

'OK, let's put it another way. You've got to work with him again and, well, I saw that script, Shannon . . .'

'Wonderful, isn't it?' Shannon asked sweetly. 'Cade gets killed in a car crash.'

'Johnny gets killed in a car crash,' Claire said carefully. 'And so does Alana. But there's a love scene first. You'll have to play it.'

'You're wrong, Claire. It's not a love scene, it's a bedroom scene. That's all they ever were. I made the mistake of thinking they were something else.' She pushed back her chair and got to her feet. 'That's next week,' she said, padding out of the room. 'I'll be fine by then.'

'Look, I'm not trying to pressure you, but that's only a couple of days from now. You make it sound as if you've got for ever to work this out.'

'There's nothing to work out,' Shannon answered, coming back into the alcove with her shoes in her hand. 'I'm an actress with a commitment to *Tomorrows*. That's all there is to it.' She bent and slipped on her high-heeled pumps. 'Didn't you just say Jerry was pleased with my work?'

'Yeah, but, well, when Morgan shows up . . . All I'm saying is it might be a good idea if you'd call him at the number he left with my secretary.'

'I have nothing to say to him, Claire. I thought you understood that.'

'I do, and I agree with you, Shannon. He's a bastard. But...'

'They haven't invented the word to describe him yet,' Shannon said sharply. 'I just wish I'd trusted my own instincts. Do you know what it's like to find out you've been used by somebody that way? I don't know which I was, an audition for *Tomorrows* or for the Hollywood movie role he wanted or... or just a diversion. Maybe it was a little of each.'

'Sweetie, don't go over all this again.'

'He knew all along that he was going to...to just walk away from me if he got the chance...' Her eyes met Claire's and she took a deep breath. 'Everything between us was a lie,' she said softly. 'Right till the end, when he handed me that story about a last-minute meeting on the Coast. No wonder he gave me that speech about *Tomorrows* and how it had been there before him and would go on after him.' Shannon stalked across the room and snatched her coat from the peg. 'That was the closest he got to the truth, but then, what if his little deal had fallen through? Suppose Scorpio had said, "No, Cade Morgan, no, we still don't want you"? Suppose they'd sent him back to New York with his tail between his legs? Why give up a sure thing in New York until you've cemented what you've got in Hollywood, right? Why not hang on to a part and a woman...'

'Hey, calm down! You've got a long day ahead of you. Don't wear yourself out before it starts.'

'Yes, you're right. What time's that audition for the Neil Simon play?'

'Three o'clock. It's a good part, sweetie.'

'Yes, but you know I'm not a comedienne, Claire.'

'Look, they want an actress, not a comic. Anyway, Papp's still interested in you for the Shakespeare Summer Festival.'

'You're leaving out the line at the employment office. I've done some of my best work there.' Shannon glanced at her wristwatch and made a face. 'Look at the time. If I don't hurry, I'll be late. And we can't have that happen, can we? After all, I'm not a big star like Mr Morgan or Rima the Prima. I've got to play by the rules.'

'We're a bit testy today, aren't we?' Claire asked quietly.

'I'm sorry,' Shannon said, hurrying back across the room and giving her agent a quick hug. 'Here I am being irritable with you when I should be thanking you for the roof over my head and a shoulder to cry on.'

Claire smiled and patted Shannon's cheek. 'Just go show the world what a pro you are, toots. That's all the thanks I want.'

An hour later, Jerry Crawford draped his arm around Shannon's shoulder.

'OK,' he said, 'we're going to tape your final confrontation with Rima. Remember, you expect trouble when she calls and asks you to meet her, OK? You don't know she's going to tell you Johnny's only been after your money, but you sense something's up. You don't like her and you don't trust her. I want you to make the audience feel your animosity. Can you do that?'

Shannon glanced past the director to where Rima the Prima stood. 'Oh, I can do that,' she said softly. 'No problem, Jerry.'

'And then we'll talk about your scenes with Cade next week, OK?'

'Jerry, believe me, I don't need a pep talk. I know you're worried about the bedroom scene, but there won't be a problem. In fact, I've already memorised my lines.'

'Good girl,' the director said, patting her on the back. 'I knew you'd come through. Right, places, everybody. Rima, are you ready?'

Shannon fluffed her hair with her fingers and then glanced down at her chalk mark. She had sounded really convincing that time—almost good enough to believe herself. Well, by Monday it would be true. When she came on the set next week, she'd be ready for Cade Morgan and that damned bed. More than ready. That bed was where everything had begun and it was where everything would end. It was time to separate reality from fantasy.

'Shannon, are you ready?'

She blinked and looked towards the control room. 'Yes, I'm ready.'

'OK, roll tape.'

Her face assumed its Alana Dunbar look as Rima began her lines in that awful voice of hers. She was as bad as ever, but that still didn't matter. She was a star, just as Cade had been. Shannon picked up her cue and fed Rima the next line. How could she had been so stupid? Falling for somebody like Cade Morgan—he hadn't even been subtle. He'd marched on to the set and into her life, taking what he wanted...

'...you won't see a penny of your inheritance, Alana,' Rima wheezed. 'My lawyers will see to it. How do you think your dear father would have felt about this disgusting relationship between you and Johnny Wolff?'

Disgusting is the right word for it, Shannon thought, moving aside so the camera could zoom in on Rima.

'He didn't want you, Alana. He was only interested in what he could get from you,' Rima purred. 'How could you have fallen for someone like him?'

'Johnny loves me,' Shannon said, feeling a kinship for Alana Dunbar that she'd never felt before. 'He said he did.'

Their lines droned on, the words and gestures almost automatic. What time was the Neil Simon audition? Not that she had a chance in a million at the part. The closest she'd come to comedy was *Twelfth Night,* which was hardly the same thing. But there were no love scenes in the Simon play, none for the *ingénue,* anyway, and that was a blessing.

How was she going to get through that love scene with Cade? At least, she didn't have to play it in that awful bodysuit. The script called for Cade to open her blouse and strip it from her. No, that was wrong. Johnny would open Alana's blouse, and Johnny would ... She crossed the set on cue, turning to the camera for her one close-up. She was going to need more than laundry lists to get her through the scene, but not because she was worried about how she'd react to Cade's touch. What she feared was that her hate would make her flinch from his caresses. That was all there was to worry about. Nothing more. Certainly nothing more.

Dear lord, was Rima going to blow her lines again? Not now, Shannon prayed, please, Rima, we're almost done. But Rima had a strange look on her face. There was a question forming in her emerald eyes as she stared beyond Shannon, no doubt looking for the cue card. Dummy, Shannon thought, it's in the other direction ...

What was happening? There was a murmur off-set, coming from behind her and now there were whispers, too. The camera was moving in for a final one-shot of Rima, but Rima was paying no attention. Hang on, Rima, Shannon urged silently, hang on. It's almost over. Just my line and then yours ...

'I'll get even with you for this,' Shannon said. It was her last line and Rima was supposed to come in on it quickly, but she was silent, standing there with her mouth agape. 'Did you hear me?' Shannon improvised. 'I'll get even ...'

Rima's glance returned to her. 'You're no good, Alana,' she said in a strange voice. 'Neither one of you, you or that rotten Joh...that John...' The emerald eyes widened until they were glowing like twin green suns. '...that Johnny Wolff,' she finally stammered, and Jerry's voice boomed from the control booth.

'Rima, damn it, what the hell's going on back there? Doesn't anybody know what "quiet" means?'

'I'm sorry, Jerry. I guess it's my fault.'

The breath caught in Shannon's throat. No, please, she thought, but even before she turned around, she knew. Cade, she thought, it's Cade.

He stood, hands planted on his hips, staring at her, his indigo eyes fathomless, his lips set in a hard line. Shannon felt as if she were replaying a scene from the past. Everything was as it had been that first day. He was dressed in leather and denim; his motorcycle boots were coated with a film of dust and for a crazy second she found herself wondering if he'd ridden his Harley here from California. There was a knot of people clustered behind him, their eyes shiny with excitement, but it wasn't Cade they were watching this time. They were watching her, trying to decide if she were to be the snake or the mongoose in what promised to be a far more interesting scene than any the writers of *Tomorrows* had ever created.

Say something, she told herself, say something nasty or say something clever, but say something. Her throat worked, but nothing happened. Her mouth was dry, her brain numb. Even her feet felt rooted to the floor.

'Hello, Shannon,' Cade said, and the sound of that familiar voice seemed to set her free.

'What are you doing here?' she said in a papery whisper.

'Working,' he said. 'That is, if you can use me today, Jerry.'

The question was directed to the control booth, but Cade's eyes never left hers.

'I—er—I don't know, Cade. I didn't expect... Just let me get out there.' The door swung open and Crawford pushed his way through the cluster of onlookers. 'I hadn't planned on shooting you two until next week,' he said, looking from Cade to Shannon. 'But we could do a rehearsal today.' His glance went from one of them to the other again, and the faintest of smiles flitted across his face. 'Why not? Have you got the script I sent you, Cade?'

'The love scene? Yeah, I've got it. It's all I thought about on the plane from LA.'

There was a titter from the crowd gathered around them. Crawford glared angrily and the noise subsided as quickly as it had begun.

'Good. Shannon? You said you'd memorised your lines, right?'

'Well, yes, but I didn't think...' Panic welled up like water from a spring. 'Jerry, look, you said Monday.'

'Monday, Friday, what's the difference?' Crawford said pleasantly. He draped his arm around her and smiled brightly. 'No problem, right?'

She nodded woodenly. 'No problem, Jerry.'

'Good. And you, Cade? Any questions about the love scene?'

'Don't worry about me,' Cade said softly, his eyes still on Shannon. 'I know every move I'm going to make.' Someone giggled again and Cade's head sprang up. 'I want the set cleared, Jerry.'

'Well, I don't know...'

'Clear it,' Cade said, his voice cutting through the studio like a whip.

Crawford waved his hand and people scuttled from the sound stage. 'OK,' he said, turning to the technicians, 'I want lights and sound on the bedroom set, please. Makeup, just dust some powder on their noses. Shannon, dear, what have you got on under that dress?'

Shannon glanced down at her costume. 'I...this is a whole Alana Dunbar outfit from Wardrobe, Jerry. A lace camisole and...'

'Fine, fine. Rima, you can take the afternoon off, if you like.'

'Certainly,' Rima said in a simpering whisper, but she only minced across the set and settled against a camera dolly. Shannon felt the colour rise to her cheeks. Rima wasn't going to pass up a chance like this.

'Jerry?' Was that tiny voice hers, Shannon wondered. She ran her tongue across her lips and tried again. 'Couldn't we just do a reading first?'

'No readings,' Cade said, rocking back on his heels. 'Let's get to it.'

He was right, Shannon told herself. Once they got past this, life could go back to normal. She could start looking for her next job and he could go back to Hollywood or Hell, whichever came first. She walked stiffly across the narrow space separating one set from the other. There was the bed, looming ahead of her, that horrible bed, that bed the size of a football field... One and one are two. Two and two are four. You can do this, she thought. Of course you can. Four and four are eight. Four is the square root of sixteen and there are four sets of sheets in the linen closet, and why in God's name hadn't she listened that time Eli had suggested that transcendental meditation was the best relaxation?

'Padgett? Are you ready?'

One last deep breath, and then she nodded and she was Alana Dunbar, walking into her gaudy bedroom, ignoring the bed which had certainly grown to a hundred miles wide and a hundred miles long. She knew what Alana would do and she did it, walking to the make-believe window, gazing out at the make-believe night, telling herself it was not Cade bursting through the door, it was Johnny Wolff, just as it was Johnny's hand on her shoulder, Johnny's fingers cutting into her flesh...

'Where the hell have you been?' he growled. 'I've been trying to find you for days.'

She turned to face him. Smile, she told herself, smile as Alana would. The Dunbar heiress was a bitch, but she was a woman, and in this scene her pride was on the line.

'I don't know why,' she said clearly, looking at Cade. 'We have nothing more to say to each other.'

'Haven't we?' he asked huskily, his gaze drifting over her. Not indigo eyes today, she thought suddenly, more like polished ebony...

'I know all about you, Johnny,' she said. 'I know everything. You were just using me.'

The words were like sand in her mouth. They're just lines, she told herself, that's all they are. They have nothing to do with you or Cade—they're Alana's words and Johnny's.

'Somebody lied to you,' Cade said, his fingers tightening on her, biting into her skin through the thin silk dress. 'I've never used you.'

Her mouth was dry, so dry... She forced herself to swallow and then she ran her tongue across her lips. 'Don't lie to me,' she whispered. 'My stepmother told me all about you.'

Cade's hand slipped to the back of her neck. 'I don't know what she told you,' he murmured, 'but it's all lies. I love you.'

You're a liar, Shannon thought, even as she said the words aloud. His hand was on the nape of her neck, splaying in her hair, his fingers rough and familiar against her skin... The script, she thought, remember the script.

'Johnny, don't,' she said, trying to say it as Alana would, trying to remember that Alana didn't really want her lover to let her go. Alana still wanted Johnny, even though Shannon didn't want Cade...

I can't, she thought, I can't. Please, don't ask me to do this. It's too much.

'I love you,' he repeated gruffly. 'You know that's the truth. Look at me, damn it! Look into my eyes.'

Slowly, her eyes met his. Was Johnny supposed to tell her to look into his eyes? She couldn't remember that in the script, but then, she was having trouble remembering lots of things. What was her next camera angle? And her next line?

'You used me,' she said again as the line tripped into her head. 'Why don't you admit it? It doesn't matter any more—it's all over. You wanted something from me and you got it.'

'OK, maybe that was part of it, at the beginning. You had something I needed. But that changed, Alana. You know it did.'

'It doesn't matter. I don't love you, Johnny.'

'You're a liar, Alana,' Cade whispered. 'A beautiful liar.'

Shannon shook her head. 'I don't love you,' she repeated as Cade drew her towards him. Dear God, that hadn't come out the way it was supposed to. Where was Alana's proud determination?

'I'm half-tempted to believe you,' Cade said, running his thumb along her cheek. 'If you loved me, you wouldn't have believed what you heard without talking to me first.'

'Nothing you can say will change anything, Johnny.'

'You don't believe that,' he said softly.

Please, she thought, please... Her heart was hammering in her ears, her blood was pounding thickly in her veins. I am Alana Dunbar, she told herself, fighting against a rising panic. I am Alana Dunbar and he is Johnny Wolff, and this is just a scene from a soap opera, that's all. It isn't anything more than that...

'Don't be afraid,' he whispered. 'You know it feels right, love.'

Something skittered wildly deep inside her. He was pulling her towards him, his arms like steel bands, and she was drowning, drowning in his eyes.

'Don't,' she said, trying to twist her face away from his, 'please...'

'I love you,' Johnny said to Alana. 'I love you,' Cade repeated softly, 'you know I love you.'

'You don't,' she gasped, 'Johnny, you don't . . .'

He was bending towards her—the script called for him to kiss her now, she thought wildly, a long, lingering kiss, and then he was supposed to fumble at the buttons of her blouse and slowly, slowly, ease it from her shoulders, his lips at the hollow of her throat.

And she would be lost. Damn him! Damn Cade Morgan, damn Jerry for making her do this. Was she supposed to make a fool of herself again? She wouldn't do it, she wouldn't, she wouldn't . . .

The crack of her hand against Cade's cheek echoed through the silent studio like a gunshot. His head sprang back; his fingers went to his face, moving lightly over the skin that already wore the red imprint of her hand. She heard Rima gasp, saw the sound man's startled face, and all the while her eyes were locked with Cade's. His eyes narrowed and darkened to a menacing vortex in the thunderhead that was his face.

'Stop it,' she said roughly. 'Just stop it! You don't know anything about love. And you never will.'

'Shannon?' Jerry's voice crackled over the microphone. 'Er—Shannon . . . I don't see any of that in my copy . . .'

There was a cackle of nervous laughter that disappeared into the ominous silence of the studio.

'That's it,' Cade growled. She flinched as he reached for her, and then he was lifting her into his arms. 'Damn it, that's the final straw.'

'You put me down,' she gasped, beating against his chest. 'Cade . . .'

'The technicians' shocked faces rolled past as Cade carried her across the studio. Jerry's voice called after them, but Cade never paused until he'd kicked open her dressing-room door and dumped her unceremoniously on her feet. 'OK,' he said roughly, 'let's get this over with.'

'It's over with, all right! If you think I'm going to stay here and play games with you . . .'

Shannon started to brush past him, but he reached out and shoved her against the wall.

'Don't push your luck,' he warned. 'I'm just waiting for an excuse.'

She lifted her chin defiantly. 'How charming,' she said. 'I didn't realise you were going to be physical. Not that I'm surprised. It goes with your motorcycle macho.'

'Where the hell have you been all week? he demanded.

'None of your business,' she snapped, trying to move past him again.

Cade smiled unpleasantly as he slammed the door shut and slipped home the bolt. 'I'm making it my business,' he said. 'And I suggest you answer the question.'

'I was right here in New York,' she said, deliberately misinterpreting his enquiry. 'Right where you left me.'

'Every day,' he said, 'every damned day, I waited to hear from you.'

'Why?' she asked sweetly. 'Did you expect a congratulatory telegram?'

'Even that would have been better than nothing.'

'OK, I apologise. Emily Post wouldn't have approved of my lack of good manners, would she? Congratulations, Mr Morgan. Enjoy your new career. Now, if you'll excuse me, we have a scene to do.'

'Forget it, Padgett. There's no way we can do that scene until we get this settled.'

Her eyes blazed with defiance. 'Why not? Can't you play it if I don't melt in your arms? Don't tell me a big Hollywood star like you needs help from little old me.'

Cade threw his head back and groaned. 'I knew it, I knew it—you're ticked off because I got a chance to make a film. I mean, what the hell, who am I to get so lucky?'

'I couldn't have said it better myself!' Shannon snapped.

'I spent the past few days going crazy, thinking about what would happen when I got here.'

'What did you think would happen when you walked out on *Tomorrows*?'

Cade's face twisted. 'I don't give a damn about *Tomorrows*,' he said. 'I'm talking about something a hell of a lot more important.'

'Of course you are,' she said nastily. 'Your wonderful new career's more important than anything else. Never mind that I'm going to end up unemployed because of you...'

'God, I don't believe it! You're jealous, aren't you? There I was, trying to find you, wondering if you'd gone crazy or been kidnapped by the gypsies, and now it turns out I could have spared myself the trouble. You were just off sulking in a corner because I got a chance you'd give your right arm for.'

'...never mind what's going to happen to *Tomorrows*' ratings...'

'Nothing's going to happen,' Cade snapped. 'They've got a juicy new storyline for Rima and some other guest star lined up. Besides, I never intended to stay for ever. Jerry and all the rest knew that...'

'...not that you care. You don't give a damn about anybody but yourself.'

'Right! That's why I spent the past three days calling Claire's office and sending you telegrams. That's why I walked out on my costume fittings and rehearsals and...'

'Why, indeed?' she purred. 'Did you realise you were in over your head?'

'I realised I couldn't go on without getting some answers from you,' he roared, shaking her roughly. 'Damn it, woman, you said you loved me...'

Shannon tossed her head to the side. 'I never did! You flatter yourself.'

'...but if you loved me, you'd have been happy for me. After all, it's not every day a movie studio asks a guy like me to step into the shoes of an actor like Jeff Anderson.'

'You don't know the meaning of love,' she spat. 'All these weeks, knowing you were going to walk out on me, using me, making me feel things I knew I shouldn't . . .' Her voice broke and she turned from him. 'How could you have done that? Flying off to LA, pretending you were going out there to talk about something that might happen months from now . . .'

'God, I couldn't believe it—there I was, packing to fly home Sunday night, satisfied that Scorpio had agreed to consider me for a film in the spring, when my agent knocks on my hotel room door and tells me Anderson's broken his leg and they want me to take his place.'

' . . . afraid to tell me the truth.' Shannon's eyes widened. 'What did you say?' she asked, turning slowly towards him.

'Can you picture it? Me, tossing stuff in my suitcase, and all of a sudden Hank says, "Unpack, Morgan. Forget that deal in the spring. You're about to make a movie now!"'

'Jeff Anderson broke his leg and you're replacing him?'

'Jesus, Padgett, how many times must I tell you? Yeah, he was skiing at Aspen and he hit a marker and smashed his leg all to pieces. How else would I have gotten a chance like this?'

Her voice was a whisper. 'You mean—they offered you the part last Sunday?'

Cade nodded his head. 'There they were, ten o'clock Sunday night, rehearsal starting Monday, filming already scheduled for Tahiti, and all of a sudden they're without a male lead. Next thing I knew, everybody was in my room, insisting I had the charisma of a Jeff Anderson, whatever the hell that means. "Are you crazy?" I said. And my agent said, "Just sign the contract before they change their minds." So I signed and then I went to call you . . .'

'To call me? Sunday night? But Claire said you signed Sunday afternoon.'

'Listen, Padgett, was Claire there or was I? I signed at eleven p.m. and I grabbed the phone so I could tell you what had happened.'

Shannon swallwoed. 'But you didn't call me.'

'Damned right I didn't. I picked up the phone and re-alised there was a three-hour time difference between California and New York. That meant it was two in the morning for you. And I thought, hell, suppose her answering machine's not on. I didn't want to wake you, not when I knew you had to be on the set early the next morning. And then I realised what a nice wake-up call my news would make. So I called the hotel desk and asked them to wake me at four in the morning. I figured I'd call you then . . .'

'That would have been seven a.m. in New York.'

He nodded. 'Right. I wanted to be your alarm clock and tell you about my contract as you opened your eyes.'

Shannon's eyes searched his. 'But you didn't,' she said softly.

'The damned hotel desk never woke me. The next thing I knew it was eight o'clock my time, which meant you were already gone for the day, so I left a message on that rotten machine of yours. I felt lousy knowing that you'd probably hear my news from somebody else first. I think I even said as much . . .'

Shannon drew in her breath, remembering the apolo-getic words he'd left on her answering machine. 'I . . . I didn't hear the whole message,' she said, picturing the plastic bits and pieces still lying in the corner of her liv-ing-room. 'My answering machine . . . broke.'

'And you never replaced it?' She shook her head and an angry scowl twisted his face. 'I thought you'd just disconnected it to avoid me. I started sending you tele-grams, but you ignored them.'

'I...I didn't get them. I've been staying at Claire's since Sunday.'

Cade scowled darkly. 'I called her office a dozen times and they wouldn't tell me where you were or how you were or...'

'Cade...' Shannon put her hands lightly on his chest. 'You mean you didn't have this Tahiti film in mind when you signed with *Tomorrows?*'

He sighed in resignation. 'Haven't you heard a thing I said? I was so worried about *Tomorrows* that the only way Crawford could talk me into signing was by agreeing to a contract I could walk away from in case I felt I was making an ass of myself.'

Shannon closed her eyes. 'A month-to-month contract,' she whispered.

'With a one-week cancellation clause,' he said. 'My security blanket, my agent called it. Crawford kept talking about a four-month storyline...'

'So did Claire.'

'I told him from day one that I might want to move on to something else if it came along. He said that was no problem. That's the best thing about soaps, he said. No character is...'

'Indispensable,' she murmured.

Cade nodded. 'Of course, that changed once I'd signed. He kept trying to pressure me into signing something long-term.' His eyes darkened and his fingers spread on her shoulders, caressing the skin beneath the thin silk dress. 'That's the only thing I feel badly about,' he said softly. 'If I'd let him pick up my option, you and I could have played Johnny and Alana a little longer. But I couldn't pass up this film, Shannon. You understand that, don't you?'

Yes, she thought, looking at him, she did. The door had opened for Cade and he had to either pass through it or watch it close in his face. That was how the theatre was. She nodded, fighting against the desire to stroke the lines of tension from his face.

'Yes, I understand. It was too good a chance to pass up.'

'Do you mean that?'

She nodded her head. 'You're a good actor, Cade Morgan,' she murmured. 'You worked hard for this opportunity.'

The tension eased from his face. 'And I owe everything to you,' he said quietly. 'You were the reason I made it.' He took her hands from his chest and clasped them in his. 'Tell me you don't hate me for walking out on Johnny and Alana.'

Don't cry, she told herself, and she shook her head. 'I could never hate you, Cade.'

'Tell me you know I'm ready for this, Padgett.'

'Of course you are,' she said carefully.

And he was, she thought. He was ready for this film, even though it would take him out of her life. But at least she knew his love had been real, even if it had only been for a little while. Nothing lasts for ever, Cade had said, but he was wrong. The memory of him would last a lifetime.

There was a knock at the door. 'Shannon? Cade? Are you ready now?'

She took a deep breath. No, she thought, she would never be ready. After they'd taped their final love scene, Cade would be gone. How would she survive a lifetime of memories?

Cade touched her cheek. 'Shannon?' he murmured.

She lifted her chin and forced a smile to her face, praying he wouldn't notice the moisture shining in her eyes. 'I'm ready,' she said. 'Come on, Johnny Wolff. Let's go out there and knock 'em dead!'

She was never going to make it. Her throat was closing and her vision was blurring...Quickly, she turned and reached for the bolt, but Cade was there first, turning her towards him with a crushing grasp.

'I don't give a damn about Johnny Wolff,' he growled.

'What?' she whispered, looking up at him. His eyes were dark with anger. 'What's the matter? I don't understand...'

'You're the one who doesn't understand, Padgett. You accused me of not being able to separate reality from fantasy. Hell, you're the one with a problem. The film and the soap are fantasy. This—you and me—this is real.'

His indigo eyes were burning into hers, demanding yet something more. What was left? A flashy finish? A crescendo of violins? 'Cade,' she said, 'I... I...' And suddenly she could no longer control herself. Tears filled her eyes. 'Damn you!' she said brokenly. 'Damn you, Cade Morgan. I've wished you well and I've smiled and I've said all the right things. What more do you want?'

His hands bruised her shoulders as he drew her towards him. 'I want you to say yes, you'll go to Tahiti with me, yes, you'll marry me...'

'What?' she said stupidly. 'What?'

Cade's arms closed around her. 'What do you think I've been talking about for the past hour? I love you, Padgett.' He shook his head at the baffled expression on her face. 'I guess I should have had a scriptwriter for this scene. All I can think of are a thousand clichés—there must be an original way to say "I love you" to the woman you want to share your life with.'

'Share you life with,' she repeated softly.

He nodded. 'We can honeymoon in Tahiti...'

'Honeymoon in Tahiti,' she sighed.

Cade grinned. 'There's an echo in here,' he said. 'Have you noticed?' He stroked the curls back from her face and kissed her lips lightly. 'It repeats everything I say. For instance, "I love you..."'

She smiled up at him. 'I love you.'

'I want to marry you.'

'I want to marry you,' she sighed.

Cade's arms tightened around her. 'You don't have to give up acting while we're in Tahiti.'

'I don't care,' she whispered, putting her arms around his neck.

'I convinced the Scorpio people to give you a part in this film.'

She sighed and laced her fingers behind his head. 'That's nice.'

Cade laughed softly. 'Don't you even want to know what kind of part it is? You won't have any love scenes.'

'Yes, I will,' she murmured, lifting her face to his. 'I'll have the only love scenes that matter.'

'For ever,' Cade whispered, and then his mouth covered hers.

Mills & Boon

YOU'RE INVITED TO ACCEPT **FOUR ROMANCES** AND A TOTE BAG **FREE!**

Acceptance card

| NO STAMP NEEDED | Post to: Reader Service, FREEPOST, P.O. Box 236, Croydon, Surrey. CR9 9EL |

Please note readers in Southern Africa write to:
Independant Book Services P.T.Y., Postbag X3010, Randburg 2125, S. Africa

YES! Please send me 4 free Mills & Boon Romances and my free tote bag – and reserve a Reader Service Subscription for me. If I decide to subscribe I shall receive 6 new Romances every month as soon as they come off the presses for £7.20 together with a FREE monthly newsletter including information on top authors and special offers, exclusively for Reader Service subscribers. There are no postage and packing charges, and I understand I may cancel or suspend my subscription at any time. If I decide not to subscribe I shall write to you within 10 days. Even if I decide not to subscribe the 4 free novels and the tote bag are mine to keep forever. I am over 18 years of age   EP20R

NAME _____

(CAPITALS PLEASE)

ADDRESS _____

_____

_____ POSTCODE _____

 # ROMANCE

Variety is the spice of romance

Each month, Mills & Boon publish new romances. New stories about people falling in love. A world of variety in romance — from the best writers in the romantic world. Choose from these titles in November.

OUTSIDER Sara Craven
LEVELLING THE SCORE Penny Jordan
JUDGEMENT Madeleine Ker
OUT OF CONTROL Charlotte Lamb
LOVESCENES Sandra Marton
NO WINNER Daphne Clair
SAPPHIRE NIGHTS Valerie Parv
CAPTIVE LOVER Kate Walker
DESPERATE REMEDY Angela Wells
ULTIMATUM Sally Wentworth
*SWEET PRETENCE Jacqueline Gilbert
*MARRY IN HASTE Carol Gregor
*EAGLE'S REVENGE Liza Goodman
*CRISPIN SUMMER Sally Stewart

On sale where you buy paperbacks. If you require further information or have any difficulty obtaining them, write to: Mills & Boon Reader Service, PO Box 236, Thornton Road, Croydon, Surrey CR9 3RU, England.

*These four titles are available from Mills & Boon Reader Service.

Mills & Boon
the rose of romance

ROMANCE

Next month's romances from Mills & Boon

Each month, you can choose from a world of variety in romance with Mills & Boon. These are the new titles to look out for next month.

AN AWAKENING DESIRE Helen Bianchin
SMOKE IN THE WIND Robyn Donald
MAN OF IRON Catherine George
RELUCTANT PRISONER Stephanie Howard
STORM CLOUD MARRIAGE Roberta Leigh
WISH FOR THE MOON Carole Mortimer
HARMONIES Rowan Kirby
LIVING DANGEROUSLY Elizabeth Oldfield
THE ORTIGA MARRIAGE Patricia Wilson
WICKED INVADER Sara Wood
*A THOUSAND ROSES Bethany Campbell
*A PAINFUL LOVING Margaret Mayo
*THE GAME IS LOVE Jeanne Allan
*CLOUDED PARADISE Rachel Ford

Buy them from your usual paperback stockist, or write to: Mills & Boon Reader Service, P.O. Box 236, Thornton Rd, Croydon, Surrey CR9 3RU, England. Readers in Southern Africa — write to: Independent Book Services Pty, Postbag X3010, Randburg, 2125, S. Africa.

*These four titles are available from Mills & Boon Reader Service.

Mills & Boon
the rose of romance

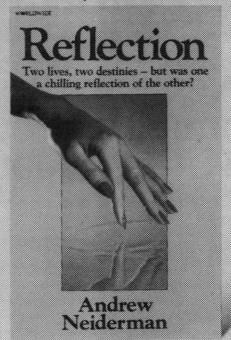